PUFFIN BOOKS

NIGHT RACE TO KAWAU

Twelve-year-old Sam is thrilled when she discovers that Dad has decided the whole family will be taking part in the night race to Kawau Island in their boat, *Aratika*. But what sounds like an exciting challenge goes drastically wrong when a gale suddenly blows up as night starts to fall, and Dad is knocked unconscious while trying to take the spin- naker down.

The author, Tessa Duder, lives in New Zealand, and readers won't be surprised to learn that she is a keen and experienced sailor and a qualified Boatmaster. Many of her summer holidays are spent sailing with her husband and four daughters in the Hauraki Gulf, where this book is set, and around the beautiful island of Kawau.

D1149125

Tessa Duder

Night Race to Kawau

PUFFIN BOOKS

Puffin Books, Penguin Books Ltd, Harmondsworth, Middlesex, England
Viking Penguin Inc., 40 West 23rd Street, New York, New York 10010, U.S.A.
Penguin Books Australia Ltd, Ringwood, Victoria, Australia
Penguin Books Canada Ltd, 2801 John Street, Markham, Ontario, Canada L3R 1B4
Penguin Books (N.Z.) Ltd, 182–190 Wairau Road, Auckland 10, New Zealand

—

First published in New Zealand by Oxford University Press 1982
First published in Great Britain in Puffin Books 1985

—

Made and printed in Great Britain by
Richard Clay (The Chaucer Press) Ltd,
Bungay, Suffolk

Contents

1. Sam goes for a run

2. Decisions at breakfast

3. A burnt pie . . .

4. . . . And a forgotten pavlova

5. Dad, but no Terry

6. Under way

7. A spinnaker start

8. Tea time

9. A wind change

10. Panic stations

11. More panic stations

12. 'Three useless kids'

13. No brandy for Sam

14. A question of responsibility

15. Shelter!

16. Bosanquet Bay

17. An apology

18. Over the top

19. Mansion House

20. Mission accomplished?

21. Saturday

Glossary

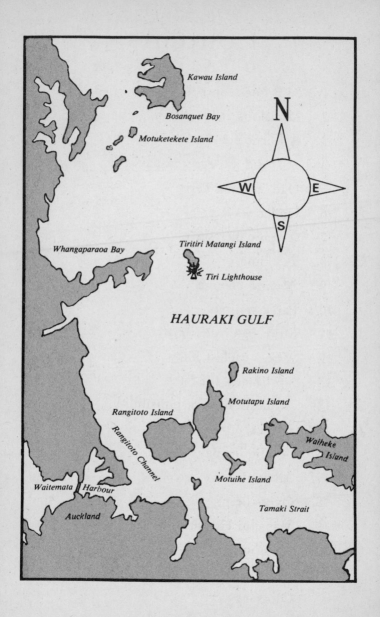

CHAPTER 1

Sam goes for a run

The old wooden stairs leading up to Sam's bedroom creaked as her father came bounding up two at a time. Sam was just awake, but she registered some haste in her father's step. This wasn't Dad with the early morning cup of tea he sometimes brought up to her; this was Dad with a message, Dad perhaps wanting a swim and a jog before breakfast.

On this particular Friday morning in February, it was Dad with a job. He shook her shoulder with more urgency than usual.

'Sam, sorry to wake you a bit early. Can you do something for me? Something that's a secret between you and me? I don't want Mum to know.'

'Depends on what it is,' muttered Sam, her eyes still closed. Like her mother, Sam wasn't good at waking up. She liked to lie in bed for a few minutes, listening to the insistent squawkings of the big black-backed gulls wheeling above the beach at the end of the road.

The early sun was shining through the turquoise and navy stripes of her curtains, casting mysterious deepwater blue shadows across her room. The curtains were the only new furnishings because most of the family's spare money went on the boat. But Sam loved her attic room. She liked to think of the other children – her father and his father before him – who had slept in the same bed and kept their clothes in the same kauri chest of drawers. They too would have been able to stand at the window in the mornings and look across the shining water to Rangitoto Island silhouetted against the eastern sky.

Mr Starr, knowing that his elder daughter took a few

minutes to get her eyes open, was shaking her shoulder again.

'Please, Sam. I want you to go along to your grandfather's place and get a key.'

'What on earth for, so early in the morning? William won't even be up.'

'Oh yes he will. He gets up at daybreak and goes for walks along the beach. He could beat you any time at getting out of bed. Anyway, we need the key for the dinghy locker for the night race tonight. I've left my key at school, and Mum will need it first this afternoon. She reminded me to bring it home yesterday, but I forgot.'

He sounded as sheepish as a small boy. I might have known, thought Sam, another conspiracy to rescue Dad from a ticking off from Mum, for leaving everything to the last minute. She smiled sleepily. There was a sound of curtains being opened and the sudden warmth of sun on her face. Then two curious words began to repeat themselves in her head.

'Night race? What was that you said? What night race?' she said, sitting up abruptly and stretching like a cat.

Her father was standing with his back to her, looking out across the sea. His voice had a keyed-up edge.

'Didn't we tell you? Oh no – we decided not to, in case the weather turned bad and we couldn't go. Tonight it's the night race to Kawau. Mum and I think you children are old enough now to crew for it, along with Terry, of course. I'm going to ring him shortly to check that he's still on.'

He turned around, his baggy pyjamas rumpled and thick curly hair sticking out so that his head, in silhouette against the window, looked enormous. Sam blinked. He looked far too big for the room. He was talking again.

'Does the idea appeal to you, Sam? It starts at six. We should arrive about midnight if the winds are as light as the forecast says they'll be. It looks pretty settled out there. I haven't done this race in years, not since we used to do it every summer when I was crewing for William. It was always a great experience. Sometimes quite hairy. Would you like to give it a go?'

'Would I ever! We've never ever been sailing at night before.' Sam leapt out of bed, hauled the still-warm bedclothes up in a single movement and pulled on an old pair of shorts and a T-shirt. This was certainly worth a jog along to William's place to get a key.

'Don't let Mum see you – or if she does, just tell her you are going for a run, which is perfectly true. I've got to get my own bag packed otherwise I'd come with you. I take it you're keen to go on the race then? It'll mean getting home promptly from school and helping your Mum with the bags and the dinghy and things . . .'

But Sam, her sandshoes hastily tied, was already half-way down the stairs and through the wide hall, tiptoeing past her parents' room. She caught a glimpse of her mother in the big double bed sipping tea with her eyes still shut. Once out the back door, she ran quickly past the three houses which stood between the Starr homestead and the beach, then turned onto the coarse sand which crunched noisily as her feet sank into it. The tide was nearly full, so she decided it would be easier to run along the concrete path under the pohutukawa trees back from the beach.

Even at this hour, Sam was by no means the first on the beach. Three old ladies in flowery swimsuits were breaststroking sedately a few metres off shore, and along the firm wet sand where the water lapped ran several joggers, muscular brown young men and thin scrawny older ones, their chests gleaming with sweat. Sam was glad she had chosen to run along the fenceline, keeping her distance from all those male bodies, even if it meant the extra concentration of keeping her rhythm on a route that went up and down several sets of shallow steps. At least she wouldn't have to say good morning.

William's place was a flat in one of the older houses up the other end of the beach. It had a verandah which looked directly northwards over the beach and across the water to Kawau Island sixty kilometres distant. Behind the house rose the smooth green hump of North Head. Standing on the verandah was like being on the bridge of a ship, which was the main reason William had moved into the flat when his wife, Sam's grandmother, had died five years earlier. Sam had been not quite seven.

Before that, he had lived in the old house where Sam and her family now lived. There had been Starrs in that house since it was built. She had vague memories of visiting her grandparents there, and of her first funeral where, try as she might, she could not associate her grandmother's frail little body with that awful shiny box covered with flowers. Not long after, saying he didn't need all that space, William had moved out of the big house.

Sam had always called her grandfather William. He would have none of that grandad, grampa or, worse, gramp and other such titles tacked onto his old mates by their descendants! And she had heard often enough, when friends inquired after him, the general opinion of him as a wise and well-adjusted old man. He had refused their offer of a self-contained room in the old house, or even building on a 'grandpa flat', saying that as long as he was able, he would manage well enough by himself; although he admitted that it was nice to have the family just up the other end of the beach. A housekeeper came once a week to clean the awkward places; and once a week he took a bus to the other side of Devonport, regardless of the weather, climbed onto the ferry and pottered over to the city to sit in a deep leather chair at his yacht club. He had been a member for fifty-nine years and there were still a few old salts left to have a yarn with. But he equally enjoyed the company of the younger members. They had a lot of time for the old man whose wealth of knowledge about ship and sail on Auckland Harbour went back to the turn of the century, and he likewise would listen for hours to their own seafaring tales.

Sometimes, in fine weather, William would get someone to help him pull the dinghy out of the locker, and then row himself out to *Aratika*. There he would haul his old limbs aboard and sit in the cockpit, puffing his pipe, fiddling with small jobs of varnishing and splicing. The whole exercise took the best part of a day but he had plenty of time. Half-forgotten memories of holiday cruises around the Gulf would drift by and he would return, tired but refreshed, to his beachside home almost as content as if he had been for a sail.

But there was one inconsistency in the picture William presented to the world of an old man who had come to terms with his advancing age – and it explained why Sam was now jogging along Cheltenham Beach to get the key for the dinghy locker.

As a young man William had worked long hours of overtime at his desk in the harbour board offices and saved hard to buy his first and only boat, *Aratika*, whose Maori name means 'direct path'. She was everything he wanted in a boat: sweet lines of kauri, nine metres long with a proud bowsprit, built by an Auckland master craftsman. Now she was nearly sixty years old, a vintage boat of character and proven seaworthiness and, like her owner, well known and respected on the harbour.

Some years earlier William had invested in a suit of modern terylene sails to replace the patched cotton ones which needed a great deal of looking after – Sam's grandmother had chosen pale turquoise for the new silky lightweight spinnaker – but otherwise *Aratika* remained what she was, a comfortable old boat. Sometimes William raced in harbour events with Sam's father Nick and some strong young friends as crew, but mostly the family just

11

cruised around the Hauraki Gulf, exploring the islands, finding new anchorages, enjoying the company of other seagoing families.

Then Sam's father had graduated from university and training college and slowly the once limitless supply of fit young men and women for crew dried up. His two sisters had married and gone overseas, Nick himself had moved around the country to various teaching posts with his new wife and young family, and over the years *Aratika* had spent more and more time bobbing at her mooring in Westhaven.

Perhaps it would have been logical, when Nick and his family came back to live in the old house, for William to come to some formal arrangement about *Aratika* with his son; sell a half share, perhaps, as he knew some other old boys did. But every time Nick raised the subject, William became unusually vague. He knew that on a teacher's salary, Nick had little enough money to spare, certainly he would never be able to buy himself a keeler. And for the present it suited William to retain the official ownership of *Aratika*. In all other respects he could adjust to the reality that he was old, and often lonely; but to give away his boat – *that* he couldn't bring himself to do. He could budget for the insurance and mooring fees. For his part, Nick and some mates did the yearly repainting job and refit, and took the old man for the occasional weekend away with the family. Both father and son were happy with the arrangement.

William had heard the young skippers in the club talking a few days earlier about the night race to Kawau, so he wasn't entirely surprised when Sam came panting up the concrete steps that led to his tiny verandah and announced breathlessly: 'William, we're going on the night race!'

'Aren't you lucky, young lady.' He smiled from the depths of a faded wooden garden chair where he had been

12

reading the morning newspaper. His wispy white hair was hidden under a floppy white hat which had seen better days, and his gnarled legs, after a summer of wearing baggy khaki shorts, were the colour of old pine-cones.

'And Dad forgot to get the key for the dinghy locker from you last night. He's left his at school, but Mum needs it first because we have to hurry down to Westhaven for the start at six o'clock, so he's sent me along to get yours so Mum won't know.' Sam sat down on the steps beside him, hugging her knees as she got her breath back after the run.

'I think I can follow you. Why doesn't he want your mother to know?'

'Well, you know, Mum can be very strict at times and she thinks Dad leaves everything to the last minute and gets everyone in a panic.'

'Mmmm – yes, I do follow you,' sighed William, remembering Nick as a small boy, then a student. He hadn't changed, despite his efficient, sometimes sharp-tongued, wife. 'The key is on the hook in the kitchen. You know the place.'

Sam fetched the key, then sat down again by her grandfather. They looked out together over the sea for a long moment. The sun was creeping up through a bright haze, throwing a silver sheen over the still water like a vast sheet of clear plastic, with the islands of the Gulf outlined in pale grey around the horizon to the east and north. Between the foreshore and Rangitoto, several dinghies and runabouts rode at anchor: early fishermen trying their luck, thought William, although he was firmly of the opinion that fishing in the Gulf was hardly worth the bother these days – not as it once was, teeming with schnapper and kahawai, John Dory and trevally, tarakihi and kingfish.

'Who's going on the night race with you?' asked

13

William presently. 'Is Jeremy going, and Jane? I hope it's not just you kids and your parents. I know it's not my business, but you never know what the weather can get up to.'

'Dad is ringing Terry this morning to check that he can come as an extra hand. You know, he's the university student who comes with us sometimes. He's still having his holidays. I don't suppose,' she added quickly, 'that Dad would want to go if Terry can't come.' She had once or twice heard William expressing doubts about the wisdom of sailing with young children on board and only one man.

'Well, it certainly looks settled enough. I heard the forecast this morning and it's for continuing fine weather. Do you think your father might ask me to come too, if Terry can't?' he asked, looking down at her with a teasing twinkle in his pale blue eyes.

'Oh yes, what a great idea! Of course he would.' Sam leapt to her feet, poised to fly off home with his request.

'No, Sam, I'm not serious, you know.' He laughed, gratified by her enthusiasm. 'I'll stick to my odd weekend. I'm too old for racing. I seem to remember having some mighty arguments with your father when we raced. He used to say I shouted at him too much. I always felt he had too much to say about how I was sailing the boat instead of getting on with his job of running the foredeck.'

He could laugh about it now, but there had been times when their arguments had become so heated that Nick had finished up saying this would be the last time he raced on *Aratika*, ever! How could he possibly trim the sails properly when the helmsman was pinching the backside off her! But it never lasted: by the time *Aratika* was sliding into the sheltered waters of Westhaven and the mooring buoy was picked up, the dispute had been long forgotten.

14

'I know what you mean,' murmured Sam thoughtfully. There was often a lot of shouting on board the yacht. Indeed, from what she gathered talking to young friends from other sailing families, there was on most yachts. Her father didn't shout much at home; there it was her mother who did any shouting that went on. She ordered people around and decided on punishments like No-Telly-For-A-Week (for really bad troubles) or No-Friends-To-Play-After-School (for minor ones). On the boat it was the other way round. Dad was the boss, standing at the tiller demanding why it was taking so long to *get that sail up*, with poor Mum muttering and flustered at the mast, juggling with bits of rope that all looked the same.

Now that she was older, Sam was beginning to make some sense of all the halyards and sheets, but Dad still got tetchy with his crew for not doing the right thing quickly enough and snapped at the two younger children, especially Jeremy, for not staying put when they were *told to stay put*! Still, Sam loved the old boat and the freedom she represented: the weekends away, the long cruise over the summer holidays in December and January. She had always supposed her mother felt the same, but now that she thought about it, Sam didn't really know whether her mother enjoyed sailing, or whether she just went along with it because of Dad's enthusiasm. She always seemed to be fussing about food, life-jackets, suncream for their noses, hats and jumpers, and lifelines when it got the slightest bit rough.

She stretched out her legs down the steps, tilting her head back and shutting her eyes to the warm sun.

'It's so peaceful here.'

'Yes, isn't it?'

'I just can't imagine that sea out there all whipped up into waves and white horses, ever again.'

The old man sighed. 'Yes, it's benign enough today.' There was another long pause, while Sam concentrated on the patterns of pink and gold from the sun shining through her eyelids. 'Your grandmother hated sailing in conditions like this, like you'll be doing tonight. She loved lots of wind and big seas, the bigger the better, well heeled over, lee rails under, lots of spray and foam.'

How very odd, thought Sam, for a woman. Her mother liked calm seas and practically no wind at all. 'Even when she was old?'

'In her last year or so, we hardly used the boat at all. And she wasn't all that old when she died, you know, although she probably seemed old to you. When we did go out for the day, it was always in mild weather. She used to hope that the wind would get up – as it often does around this coast in the late afternoons.' He chuckled. 'Even though she was hardly strong enough to tie a knot, she used to insist on letting the jib sheets go and would have winched in the leeward jib sheets if I'd let her. It was all a matter of timing, she used to say, not brute strength. She was right too, up to a point. But I always took at least two crew, usually three. You and your parents were down south then.'

He took a long puff at his pipe, while Sam's eyes followed the path of a small coastal tanker which had drawn around North Head on its way out to sea. Over by the Rangitoto lighthouse she could see the white pilot launch waiting patiently to take off the pilot.

'We had some pretty hairy night races to Kawau too, as I recall. Winds right on the nose and the main reefed right down. Rain so thick you couldn't see a thing. No one had liferails around their decks in those days, or pulpits, or wore lifelines or even life-jackets much, either. I suppose it was a miracle we never lost anyone over the side in that race. Of course the fleet was much smaller, not the hundred-odd that will go off tonight.'

'I wouldn't like to be at sea in a storm at night,' said Sam. More accurately, she would be terrified. It was bad

16

enough the few times they had been caught in bad weather during daylight.

'I've been afraid, once or twice.' Sam waited, but her grandfather didn't seem inclined to elaborate.

Below the verandah, the gentle sea rippled and lapped against the high-water mark. There, quite clearly laid out, was the course they would be taking tonight, through the Tiri passage then on to Kawau just visible between Tiri and the mainland. A piece of cake, as Dad would say. A breeze! Yet there was something sinister about the very stillness of the water. She looked up at the clear blue morning sky for reassurance.

'You'll have no worries about the weather tonight, young Sam,' said William, reading her thoughts. 'Your father's a good seaman. A good navigator, too.'

'I know. He's started to teach me navigation,' said Sam proudly, glad that the conversation had swung away from veiled references to the dangers of sailing.

'Has he now?' William sounded impressed. 'You know about variation and deviation and all that junk?'

Sam laughed. 'You sound like the boys at school.'

'Never! I remember your father at intermediate school age. The language!'

'Dad?' One thing about Dad: he might shout on board the boat, but he hardly ever swore. 'I bet he wasn't as bad as the boys in my class. He couldn't have been.'

'Maybe not. Your grandmother was a very tolerant lady, but even she found that stage trying.'

'You know, William, I can't remember grandmother very well. She was always sitting on the verandah of the big house drinking tea when we came to visit, with that old crochet rug over her knees. She had big brown eyes like . . . like wet stones on the beach.'

'She was sick even then. But her eyes never lost their sparkle, true. You were only a baby.'

'I had started school! I was seven when she died.'

17

'Still a baby.' They laughed.

'She must have been a character. Especially if she liked sailing in stormy weather. I don't think most women do.' Sam had hardly ever heard William talk about her grandmother before.

'She was.'

Sam bent down to kiss the old man. He seemed to have forgotten she was there. She said gently, 'I'll come and see you on Sunday night and tell you all about it. Do you know, we've never actually been sailing at night.'

'Ah, you have an experience in store, young Samantha. On a quiet night, it's like fairyland. Dozens of little toy boats, lit up like Christmas trees, sailing into the sunset.'

He took a long pull at his pipe. 'Don't forget the key.'

But Sam, the key safely in her pocket, was already down the steps and on the sand, her long fair hair streaming out behind as she ran back to breakfast.

CHAPTER 2

Decisions at breakfast

Sam came crashing in through the back porch just as her mother appeared in the kitchen to get breakfast, dressed like Sam in a pair of old shorts, a T-shirt and bare feet. She looked more like a big sister than a mum, thought Sam – except for the dark smudges under her eyes.

'Here's our baby ballerina again,' said Mrs Starr, getting out a huge jar of home-made muesli. 'Just in time to set the table. Have you been for a run?'

'Just along to William's place to tell him about the night race,' said Sam, conscious of the key tucked in her shorts pocket. 'At first he wanted to know if he could come too, but then he said he was only teasing and he was too old for racing.'

'Yes. Your father has just informed me we are going on the race,' said Mrs Starr.

'You don't sound very pleased about it. Don't you want to go?' asked Sam, puzzled at her mother's tone. 'I think it's a terrific idea.'

'I don't know. I think you're still a bit young to go racing at night, even in good weather. I can't say I'm bursting with enthusiasm. I have work this morning and I'll be hard pushed to get everything ready before we leave the mooring in time for a six o'clock start.'

She lined up four lunchboxes and aimed a tomato into each. 'But Dad's all keyed up, and barring a major calamity, there's no stopping him now. He's just ringing Terry to check he's coming. Get the egg-cups out, will you, Sam? And please don't rattle around in the cutlery drawer any more than you have to.'

19

Sam picked out the knives and egg-spoons as quietly as she knew how, feeling deflated and vaguely guilty.

'You'd better go and have a shower and get your uniform on,' continued her mother. 'I hope to goodness it's clean, as your other one isn't ironed. And get your sailing bag packed before you go to school, please. We'll have little enough time when we get home.'

Sam knew exactly what this entailed, as Mrs Starr had long ago insisted that the three children take responsibility for their own gear. Togs, two towels, two pairs shorts, one pair jeans, one skivvy, two T-shirts, two jumpers, parka, sandshoes, pyjamas, toothbrush and a couple of paperbacks to read; all in a stout heavy-duty plastic bag that wouldn't immediately let in water if dropped in the tide.

'My bags are in the hall. Get one of the kids to help you take them out to the car later,' said Mr Starr, making a big blustery entrance into the kitchen. 'Good morning, Sam. I've just got through to Terry, Mum. He says he'll meet you at the dinghy lockers just after four. You can stow the boat and get the sails bent on, and then all you have to do is pipe me aboard at five o'clock.'

Sam knew he was teasing, but her mother's face remained stony as he went on. 'I may not be able to make it earlier, as I've a staff meeting after school.'

'Yes, cap'n, *sir*,' replied Mrs Starr sarcastically, slapping butter on the rolls for lunch. 'And while you're spending a nice relaxed day teaching, I've got work this morning and then shopping and packing up the food and locking up the house, and making sure the kids haven't forgotten anything, and driving to Westhaven in the rush-hour traffic and parking the car and getting the dinghy out and loading all the gear and rowing out to the boat. Then you step on board and say "anchors away"!'

Sam busied herself in the pantry, out of firing range.

'Come on, love,' said Mr Starr reproachfully, looking

up from tying his shoelaces. 'Look, I know you take the brunt of the preparations, but there's no way I can change that. You've done this dozens of times. What's the difference between going on this race, which happens to start at six o'clock, and just going away for the weekend as we usually do on Fridays? You don't make such a hoo-ha about it then. We're supposed to be doing this for pleasure. R and R as they say in the Navy.'

'Don't be flippant, please, Nick,' said Mrs Starr. She put down the knife and sighed heavily, pushing back the short hair from her forehead. 'I don't know. I just feel uneasy about the whole thing. The kids are too young, and it puts too much pressure on us all.'

'But we talked about this earlier in the week. You seemed keen then.' Sam's father seemed at a loss. 'Surely . . . Now I know it's not my business even to suggest how you organize your time but . . .'

'That's right.'

'But you have got three hours when you get back from work before the kids come in. Your schedule isn't that tight.'

'It's not . . .'

'And you and Terry make a perfectly adequate crew for tonight's weather, kids or no kids.'

'I'm crew,' put in Sam indignantly, from the pantry.

'You're crew,' replied her father in mock courtesy. He turned back to the fray. 'No spinnakers either, unless we're just ghosting along.'

There was a pause, while Mrs Starr tore off strips of lunch paper to wrap the filled rolls. Finally she said, 'What is the forecast?'

'Light south-easterlies, continuing fine. Seas slight. Perfect for you, Mum! Come on, I appreciate you'll be tired by the time I arrive, but we'll have the gentlest of races and we'll all try to give you a good rest tomorrow.'

The only sound in the sunny kitchen was the bubble of

boiling water in the egg saucepan. Sam thought it safe to emerge from the pantry; she supposed her mother was resigned to the race, since her expression was impassive. Dad, having received the slightest of nods to indicate her grudging acquiescence, had disappeared to have a shave.

'You've got black rings under your eyes, Mum,' said Sam in what she hoped was a sympathetic voice.

'I always find the first week back at work a strain, Sam. And I didn't sleep very well last night.' She changed the subject abruptly. 'You'd better get those other two down for breakfast. And turn the stove off. It's too soon to put the eggs in yet.'

'Why didn't you sleep well? You usually sleep like a log.'

'Dreams.'

'What about?' persisted Sam.

There was a slight pause.

'Waves,' said her mother briefly, avoiding Sam's eyes as she put a completed lunch on top of Dad's briefcase. 'Big green waves.'

'Well, there won't be any big green waves tonight,' said Sam lightly. 'The sea is like a millpond.' Yet a vague sense of unease was creeping back into her mind. It was a feeling she didn't understand; they were a sailing family, they had just been away cruising to the Bay of Islands for a whole month, so why should the night race to Kawau be any different? Dad wouldn't even have to get out the charts, just follow all the other boats straight into Bon Accord Harbour.

'It's a quarter past seven, Sam. Please get Jeremy and Jane down for breakfast, and give Dad a shout.' Her mother's voice was polite but remote. That, for the moment, seemed to be the end of the matter.

Climbing thoughtfully up the stairs, Sam tried to rekindle her own earlier enthusiasm. The sound of raised voices

22

told her that Jane was annoying Jeremy in his room, further along the passage.

'Hey, you guys. Mum says get cracking and get your sailing bags ready. We're doing something special this weekend. The night race. To Kawau.'

Jeremy was sitting up in bed, trying to push Jane off the other end with his feet.

'Get *off*, you great lump, go sit somewhere else. Better still, shove off into your own room and take that cat with you.'

'No, why should I?' Jane, with the family cat Stormy draped over her shoulder, sat grimly on the heaving bed. 'If you'd let me have that book in the first place, I would have gone by now. Go on, you've finished it, so why can't I have it?'

Sam saw that Jeremy was hugging a book to his chest, his face determined.

'Because I have to take it back to the school library, that's why,' he said triumphantly.

'Well, renew it then. Anyway, you can't need to take it yet,' went on Jane scornfully. 'We've only been back at school a week.'

Jeremy had opened his mouth to reply when he noticed Sam in the doorway and heard her second attempt to break into the conversation.

'Hey, you guys, stop it, will you? Didn't you hear what I said? We're going night racing.'

They both looked at her, suddenly silent.

Sam went on. 'Mum says get up and get your sailing bags ready because we have to leave as soon as we get home from school and the race starts off Orakei wharf at six o'clock.'

She went over to pull up the blinds. There was a faint smell of dust and warm bodies.

'Gosh, how can you sleep with the window shut, Jeremy? No wonder this room stinks.'

'It doesn't.'

'You're so used to it you can't smell it.'

Jeremy decided to ignore this. 'They don't have races at night. You couldn't see the marker buoys, for one thing.'

'Little boy, they do have one race at night, only we've never heard about it because you've not been old enough to go,' replied Sam.

'That's not my fault,' said Jeremy briskly.

'So now you're old enough, Dad says we can go on the race provided Terry can come too. And haven't you ever heard of lighthouses?'

Jeremy fell silent, feeling rather foolish. He couldn't be bothered arguing with both Jane and Sam. But now that he thought about it, he didn't much like the idea of racing at night when you couldn't see where you were going, lighthouses or no lighthouses.

'I don't think I want to go,' he said loftily. 'I'll go and stay with Andrew.'

'Don't be so wet,' said Jane, staring out the window, her mind dreaming up images of lighthouses, great curling waves rushing at them in the darkness, red sunsets and lots of stars. She was remembering the times when she woke on *Aratika* and needed to go out into the cockpit to use the bucket. Usually other yachts would be anchored nearby, their riding lights swinging, with faint flapping and pinging noises echoing, even on very still nights, like some ghostly orchestra tuning up.

Sam was speaking. 'Andrew's Mum won't want you for the whole weekend. She's got five kids already.'

'She always says one more doesn't make any difference.'

'Well, you can't just invite yourself; and anyway, you know how disappointed Dad would be. He's really keyed up about it. You can't not come.'

'Why can't I not come?' persisted Jeremy. 'I'm sick of sailing. We've just had the whole holidays away.' He pulled on his jeans sullenly. 'I wish I belonged to a normal family that wasn't always sailing about in a boat. Every time something exciting happens I get shouted at to sit down, and I know just as much about sailing as Jane.'

Sam looked down at her nine-year-old brother. First a reluctant mum, now Jeremy; she was tired of listening to people being negative. She wondered what Jane's reaction would be when she stopped staring out the window, but apparently Jane had been listening. She turned around and regarded Jeremy with some disdain.

'No you don't. You can't tie a bowline, let alone a sheet-bend, and you're not strong enough to winch in the jib sheets. Anyway, think how lucky we are to have a boat at all, especially one big enough for all of us. I have lots of friends whose fathers go off sailing every weekend and leave them at home to muck around by themselves.' She marched decisively out of the room.

'I'll teach you to tie a bowline tomorrow – or even on the race tonight if it's as calm as Dad says it will be,' offered Sam. 'Jeremy, Mum's being all lukewarm about the race too. I think Dad might throw a wobbly if you start as well.'

'Okay, okay.' He began to thrust clothes into his sailing bag, as a call came clearly from downstairs. 'Isn't anyone coming to breakfast? It's half past seven and we're *all* going to be late for *everything*.'

Two minutes later, Mr Starr and the three children were sitting at the breakfast table.

'I hope all your sailing bags are ready,' said their mother. 'I'm sorry the eggs will be a bit overdone, but you all took so jolly long to get here.'

'But I hate hard eggs,' wailed Jane.

'I can't help that. It's good protein, so please get on with it. Or empty your egg out into the saucer and mash it up with butter for a spread on your toast. Either way, I don't care, so long as it's eaten.'

'Look at that. Hard as a rock,' muttered Jane, prising off the lid.

'Jane, stop grizzling. Jeremy, will you sit down! What do you want?'

'The salt. Sam didn't set the table properly. She never does.'

Sam opened her mouth to protest, but her mother was quicker.

'Jeremy, don't you say another word. And don't put too much salt on that egg. It's not good for your insides. Hardens your arteries.'

'But I like the taste of salt.'

'You're not eating salt, you're eating an egg,' said Sam.

'Nick,' Mrs Starr interrupted, 'hadn't you better tell the children about tonight?'

'Oh, yes. Here's the key for you, Mum, before I forget.' Sam had just managed to slip it across the table before her mother came over with the eggs. He gave her an appreciative smile. 'I've already told Sam,' he said to Jane and Jeremy. 'We thought we'd do the night race to Kawau tonight. A six o'clock start, which means a slightly earlier getaway than usual. We'll have to drop the mooring by five-fifteen at the very latest, in time to be at Orakei before six.'

'Will we see phosphorescence and things?' asked Jane, still busily mashing her egg to a paste.

'Should do. It really won't be much different from our usual Friday sail, just longer, and we'll be sailing at night, which will be a new experience for you. Don't get too excited, though – if there's not much wind, you younger ones will sleep most of the way. Last year there was no breeze at all to speak of, and the fleet trickled in to Mansion House just before dawn.'

'What's so special about the night race to Kawau?' said Jeremy. Sam looked up warningly from her egg.

'Jeremy doesn't want to come,' said Jane flatly.

'How do you know that?' asked Mr Starr.

'Sam told us before. Jeremy said he was sick of sailing.'

'Jane, I think you're stirring up trouble,' said Mr Starr mildly. 'I know we've had a lot of sailing lately, what with the Christmas holidays and the Anniversary Regatta last week. I think your Mum's feeling a bit the same way.'

'Well, what is so special?' continued Jeremy, carefully placing his empty eggshell upside down in the cup.

His father pushed back his chair from the table. 'There is something special about being at sea after dark. And it's the only event in the racing calendar, apart from the big ocean races around the coast, which sets off at sundown. There'll be well over a hundred boats.'

There was a brief silence. Looking round at the three thoughtful children, Mr Starr felt obliged to continue.

'They've been holding this race nearly every year since about 1931. I suppose the magic of Kawau is part of it. Sir George Grey made Mansion House famous all over the world, you know.'

'You're beginning to sound as if you're giving a history lesson,' said Mrs Starr, putting a large mug of coffee in front of him. 'The children know all that.'

Sam looked quickly at her father; if that remark had been aimed at her, she would have felt put down.

'Mum, I was only trying to answer Jeremy's question. Perhaps I haven't explained very convincingly, but there *is* something special about this race.'

'I'm looking forward to it, Dad,' soothed Sam.

'Me too,' added Jane quickly. 'Jeremy's only being wet.'

'Jane, will you let Jeremy speak for himself?' There was an edge to his normally mild voice. About time, too, thought Sam. Jane's too prone to minding other people's business for them.

27

'Is Terry coming with us?' asked Jeremy. If there was no way he could avoid the race, at least it would be nice to have another male on board. There were too many females in this family.

'Yes – he's meeting you at the dinghy lockers at four. You've all got to get home smartly from school and help Mum. Is there anything else the children can do before they go to school?' he inquired of his wife's uncommunicative back at the sink.

'I don't think so, as long as they tidy their rooms, shut the windows, pull the curtains and put their sailing bags in the car. Clear all the dishes off the table, please, as you go.' Sam winced as the egg saucepan clattered loudly into the sink. 'Sam, it's your turn to dry the dishes. Nick, hadn't you better go and catch that bus?'

She suddenly saw Jeremy's apparently uneaten egg perched innocently on the wooden egg-cup. 'So help me, if Jeremy hasn't left his egg after all that. Come back here, young man,' she shouted into the hall, 'and finish this egg up.'

Jeremy's face peeped grinning from behind the pantry door. 'Tricked ya, Mum.'

Mrs Starr seemed to have difficulty in taking the joke. 'Get out of here, will you, before I blow my cool.' He went, fast.

'Poor mum,' said Sam, keeping her smiles to herself. 'Why did you have to go and have a boy?'

'Ask your father.' Her voice was brusque, but Sam could see a faint twitch to her mouth as she squirted the washing-up liquid into the sink of hot water. 'And talking about your father,' she added, raising her voice, 'he's going to miss his bus if he messes around in the porch cleaning shoes much longer. Please Nick, I don't want the added complication of having to run you to the ferry. Not today. Please.'

'Coming, coming.' Mr Starr burst out of the porch,

swallowed the rest of his coffee, picked up his briefcase and crammed his carefully packed lunch among the papers. 'Give me a ring at lunch time if you have any problems,' he said, planting a kiss somewhere near his wife's right ear and ruffling Sam's hair in a passing gesture of farewell. 'Otherwise I'll meet you at the boat, five at the latest. If you and Terry are ready before then, you can engine over to the ramp and pick me up there. It'll save a bit of time.'

Mrs Starr nodded, preoccupied with the dishes. 'Righto. Have a good day at school,' she said absently.

'Bye Dad,' called Sam as her father hurtled out the back door and ran along the path outside the kitchen window. They could hear the bus grinding its gears as it came around the corner at the end of the road. As usual, he would make it – but only just.

'Thank goodness he's gone! I can't think with so many people around.' Mrs Starr was briskly wiping the toastcrumbs off the table, but there was nothing brisk about her voice. 'Now, let's see. Food for the weekend, work this morning, my head's spinning. Is that all the dishes, Sam?'

'Mum, if you really don't want to go tonight, why didn't you suggest that Dad went with Terry and William and some other men? I know William would go like a shot. I wouldn't mind staying at home, and Jane too, and Jeremy for certain wouldn't mind.' She hoped she sounded convincing.

'Sam, I know it sounds silly in a city the size of Auckland to say you can't find unattached men to go on a yacht race, but really, it's not so easy. Most skippers have their crews lined up well in advance, and if they are married they can't just leave their families at a few hours' notice.'

'But just for one weekend. You wouldn't mind, would you?'

29

To her astonishment, her mother began to smile. The first real smile that morning. It was like the sun coming out.

'Ah – my dear Sam – when you are older and have a husband of your own, I wonder how you'll work out the problem. I wonder if you'll be as lucky as me.'

'What problem? And why are you lucky?'

'This weekend there will be hundreds of yachting widows left at home, looking after the kids, carting them round to tennis and music lessons and Sunday school, cooking, washing, ironing, picking up things off the floor, just like any other day of the week. And there's not only yachting widows. Think of all the golfing widows, and handyman widows whose husbands spend all weekend building boats or rumpus rooms or painting everything in sight.'

'Well,' said Sam emphatically, 'when I'm married we shall go sailing together at the weekends.'

'What about when you have a baby to look after? Or two? Or even three?'

'I'm only going to have two children. And we'll take them with us.'

Her mother was chuckling. 'Good luck to you, Sam.'

'Mum, what's the point of all this? You haven't sat at home while Dad went sailing, neither have we.'

'Yes, and that's why I say I'm lucky, because Dad is just as happy to potter round the Gulf with his family. In fact, he prefers it. But I know quite a few family men with children your age who go off racing as regular crew on the big yachts. Marvellous relaxation after the pressures of work. Salt air, the great outdoors! Getting away from it all, and that includes their families. I'm not saying it's necessarily wrong. Each family has to work out these things for itself. But there seems to be a tradition that men can do it and women can't, even on rare occasions. What do you think about that?'

Sam thought. 'I suppose,' she said, carefully drying the saucepan, 'I'd be a bit jealous being left at home, because I like sailing too. But we could take it in turns.'

'Yes, you could.' She was smiling again.

'Mum, I still don't see what all this has to do with going on the night race.'

'Simply – that I should be counting my blessings for having a husband who actually wants to take his family along. I know I'm sometimes tough on your poor father, but at least I'm not being left behind on the wharf waving a handkerchief. So I really shouldn't be carrying on, should I? That's all the dishes, thanks.'

Mrs Starr gave Sam a spontaneous kiss on the top of her head. 'Goodness, you are getting tall. I had to tiptoe to do that. Sometimes I need someone like you, Sam, to point out the obvious. I still feel that Jeremy is a bit young for night racing, you're all a bit young, but with the weather so settled – well, I suppose it's okay.'

When her mother smiled, all the world was happy. Sam felt as though a burden had been lifted. She gave her mother a quick hug.

'Must go for my bus.'

'Got your lunch?'

'Yep. Bye, Mum. Have a good day.'

'You too. And remember to hurry home after school,' she called. With any luck she might get a few moments to collect her thoughts before Jane and Jeremy came clattering back to collect their lunches and say goodbye. And after that: preschoolers at the kindergarten where she worked five mornings a week. Today they would be making pikelets. She began to gather the milk and other ingredients she would need. She would have to worry about food for the weekend later.

CHAPTER 3

A burnt pie . . .

A burnt bacon and egg pie gives off a most pungent smell – a
smell like sulphur and old gumboots. Sam's nose began to
twitch even as she hurried along the road from the bus; the
closer she got to the house, the stronger it seemed to get.
Then, passing the kitchen window, she saw smoke
billowing round the hibiscus and oleander bushes outside.

She dropped her bags inside the gate and ran. The smell
and the smoke became overpowering as she peered into
the kitchen and heard the oven timer ringing. Where was
Mum? Why wasn't she here? 'Mum? Mum!' she yelled.
There wasn't a sound from the big old house.

The smoke was coming from the oven but there were
no flames. It seemed to be thicker nearer the ceiling so,
stooping low, Sam charged into the kitchen and flung
open the oven door. Frantically waving her arms in front
of her, she tried to see what was inside. The element at the
bottom was glowing red-hot. That's it – turn the oven off.
She turned it off at the wall for good measure. The timer
stopped. Coughing, she shut the oven door, uncertain
what to do next. It was probably better to take the burnt
whatever-it-was outside, so she opened the door again
and felt around inside with the oven cloth. She carefully
grasped the smoking pie-dish with both hands,
straightened up and ran for the back door. She could feel
the heat seeping through the thick cloth. It became too
much. She dropped the lot, all over the back porch.

Oh, Mum! The pie-dish, with thick flakes of charred
pastry and blackened remains of egg, lay smoking on the
mat. Now it would burn holes. She grabbed the cloth,
then the dish and flung everything out on the concrete.
Tears of relief and rage filled her eyes. Where on earth was

Mum? She shouldn't be expected to cope with a fire after school – or a near fire.

Wiping her eyes, Sam bent down and threw the remaining pieces of black pastry onto the path. The smoke still hung heavily in the kitchen. Perhaps if she opened the front door a breeze would blow through. But the air was too still; the puriri and big pohutukawa in the front garden barely stirred. Then she remembered the race. Of course, the bacon and egg pie had been to take on board the boat for tea. She looked at her watch. Half past three. Where was Mum? They had to leave in half an hour.

Then she heard the car, being driven faster than usual, come down the road, bounce with a squeal of protesting brakes over the kerb and skid to a halt in the drive. If she hadn't known it was her mother and the family car, she would have thought it was one of those yahoos who drove down to the beach in souped-up cars with fat tyres and half the engine showing. Seconds later, the key turned in the lock and her mother dashed in through the front door.

'It's all right, Mum. I've put out the fire,' said Sam, standing in the hall and feeling more than a little pleased with herself. Her mother headed straight on towards the kitchen.

'I said, I've put it out!' said Sam, following. 'The pie is outside the back porch. It won't be any good to eat, that's for sure.'

Her mother was surveying the open oven door and the trail of blackened pastry. She waved her arms to dispel the lingering smoke and turned around to where Sam was standing uncertainly in the doorway; there was no sign of gratitude or relief in her expression, just annoyance.

'Where was the fire?'

'Well, there wasn't one really. Only smoke, but so much of it you couldn't see the other side of the kitchen. I turned off the oven and took the pie outside. It's out on the path. Where *were* you, Mum?'

Mrs Starr didn't say anything. Instead she filled the hot-water jug for a cup of tea as though her life depended on it.

'Phew, what happened?' said Jane cheerfully, walking into the kitchen. 'What a terrible smell.' She heaved her schoolbag onto the table.

'Jane, take that bag to your room, get changed and start taking the things out to the car,' said her mother. 'You too, Sam. We're supposed to leave in twenty minutes.'

'Mum,' Sam persisted, ignoring Jane. 'Where were you? Where have you been?'

'At the boring old doctor's, that's where,' said Jane. 'Jeremy got a cut on the head at school, so Mum had to come up and get him, but he doesn't need stitches and the doctor says he can go sailing as long as he's kept quiet.'

'Jane, *please* go and get changed.'

'What can I have to eat?'

'Nothing. We haven't got time.'

'But I'm starving.'

'Jane, for pity's sake. We'll get some chocolate or biscuits or something on the way. Go and get ready.'

'A drink then.'

'There's milk in the fridge.'

'Milo?'

'Jane, if you push me any further, I'll scream,' said Mrs Starr.

'Okay,' said Jane unperturbed, pouring a huge glass of milk from the bottle and draining it. 'I'm going. I'm gone.'

'Thank goodness for that. Without washing her glass either,' muttered Sam. She was feeling hungry too, but she didn't dare ask if there were any biscuits in the tin. Her mother was busy wiping out the oven with a dishcloth. Sam got out two tea bags and made the tea.

'Here, Mum. Want anything to eat?'

'No, thanks.' She stood up, waving her arms around. 'We'll just have to wait until Monday to air the place out properly.'

'Mum, is that really what happened? Is Jeremy all right?'

34

'I got a call from school to take him to the doctor. He got pushed over. It's only a superficial cut.'

Mrs Starr pushed back her hair, shutting her eyes wearily. 'I had a heavy morning at work. Then two mothers were late picking up their kids, full of excuses as usual. I know they're both solo mums and have to work but they forget I'm a working mum too. When I got the call from school, I'd just thrown the pie in the oven. I clean forgot about it. And of course we had to wait twenty minutes at the doctor's.'

'Well, it could have been worse. Like stitches. Can I have a biscuit?' she slipped in nonchalantly.

'Yes. Oh, sure, I might be sitting at the hospital now, reading two-year-old magazines while we wait three hours for two stitches.' She drained her tea. 'Or we might have had a fire. Those dishes will have to wait until Sunday night. Where did you say you'd taken the pie?'

'I threw it outside. I don't think you'll ever get the dish clean.'

'Turf the whole thing into the rubbish tin then. We'll have to get some fish and chips on the way over to Westhaven. You'd better go and get changed, Sam, and help Jane with those things in the hall. Jeremy is asleep on the back seat of the car. *Don't* wake him, please.'

Not a word of thanks, thought Sam. Just orders and sighs. If it hadn't been for me, Mum, she shouted silently, the whole place might have gone up in flames. She thumped down the back steps and picked up the pie-dish. It was still hot, but holding it by the edges she managed to get it into the rubbish tin. Then she ran up to her room and pulled off her uniform, kicking it into a heap by the window. She could hear orders being barked at Jane downstairs, then louder still: 'Sam, are you *ready*?'

She pulled on the same T-shirt and shorts she had worn in the morning and took a quick look at the sea before running downstairs. Despite her annoyance with Mum, she was excited. Soon, none too soon, they would be out of this house and on their way to Kawau.

35

CHAPTER 4

. . . And a forgotten pavlova

Mrs Starr started up the engine. Equally decisively, she switched it off again and sat staring at the house.

What's wrong *now*? thought Sam.

'I've checked the house. We've got the chilly bin, five sailing bags, three life-jackets. Did you put *five* sailing bags in the car, Jane?'

'I think so,' said Jane sullenly from the back seat which was largely occupied by her sleeping brother.

'You think so. I hope you're right. And where's the cat?'

'Here, under my feet,' said Jane.

'Well, where's his box?'

'In the back.'

'I'm not leaving here until that cat is safely in his box,' said Mrs Starr leaping out of the car. She pulled up the big rear door of the station wagon. 'Now that I'm here we may as well check the gear again. Five sailing bags, yes. Chilly bin, life-jackets, yes. The cat's box – here, pass him over, Jane.'

She took the reluctant Stormy and put him firmly in the cat box, fastening the lid swiftly before he had a chance to poke his head up. Sam felt sorry for the poor cat; she knew he fretted inside his box.

'Right,' sighed Mrs Starr, once again starting up the engine. 'Now perhaps we can go.'

'Money for fish and chips, Mum?' came Jane's voice from the back.

'Always thinking of your stomach,' said Sam.

'That's enough, Sam. The answer, Jane, is yes I have some money. There'll be no more talk unless it's kind, interesting or informative.'

The traffic lights turned red all along the way as if to spite them. Even the fish and chips, which Mrs Starr had ordered by phone, seemed to take longer than usual.

'Terry will be waiting at the dinghy lockers, wondering where the devil we are,' said Mrs Starr, looking at her watch as they waited for the green arrow into the bridge approach road. Sam knew her mother was a very punctual person.

They took the outside lane over the bridge. Sam looked eagerly down at the yacht basin at the other end of the bridge were *Aratika* was moored. Yes, she could see their boat over towards the southern edge of the basin where there was a jumble of shipyards and a few sad-looking ferries. Her eye picked out the bright orange trimaran which she knew was just in front. Even now a steady succession of keelers was chugging under motor out through the breakwater and heading down the harbour towards Orakei. As Dad had taught her, she looked down over the busy harbour with her weather eye: checking the surface of the water (slightly ruffled), any smoke from the port area (none today), any boats under sail (only one, moving along gently on a reach), and using burgees on moored boats as wind indicators (just enough to shake them into shape).

'Mum, we're not going to make it to the start, are we,' said Jane suddenly: a statement, not a question. Sam both envied and resented the way her younger sister tended to organize the family.

'Yes we are,' said Sam quickly. 'We've got to. Dad will be awfully disappointed if we don't.'

'I agree we're cutting it fine,' nodded Mrs Starr, skilfully manoeuvring the car through the heavy Friday afternoon traffic. She bumped, faster than Dad ever did, over the judder bars past the club-houses. In the back, Jeremy stirred and groaned.

'Hey, watch it, Mum,' said Jane.

'Well, it's after half past four,' said Mrs Starr, swinging the car into the loading bay near the dinghy lockers where a white Mercedes, a Jaguar and other expensive-looking cars were already parked.

'I can't see Terry here,' said Sam ominously. With Terry to help, Mum's mood would certainly improve; it always did with another adult around – apart from Dad, that is, who sometimes seemed to have the opposite effect.

'He'll turn up,' said Mrs Starr peevishly as she opened the rear door and swiftly unloaded the bags onto the footpath.

Sam, standing uncertainly by the open door of the car, searched for Terry's stocky frame among the busy, preoccupied people coming and going around her, carrying gear, unloading cars, lifting dinghies, looking important. There were two or three families dressed for sailing like themselves but mostly there were men looking as smug, thought Sam, as schoolboys wagging school. She caught the heavy perfumed air surrounding a small cluster of wives standing nearby, immaculate in their smart clothes. Sam stared. Anything less like her own mother in denim shorts, bare feet, and short haircut she couldn't imagine. Mum was going sailing; they were presumably going home. But to what? What would expensive ladies like that do all weekend, with no houses to paint, boats to sail, housework to do, or gardening . . .

'Come on, girl,' her mother's voice interrupted. 'No time to stand and stare. You and Jane start getting the dinghy out while I park the car.' With a sideways glance at the waiting women and the faintest glimmer of a smile on her face, Mrs Starr handed Sam the key.

'Good that Dad remembered his key for once,' her mother was saying. 'Or is that why you went along to William's this morning?'

'How did . . .?' Sam began, but Mrs Starr had already banged the car door shut and started up the engine.

The Starr family wagon backed out of the loading bay, narrowly missing the white Mercedes which was also leaving. Sam watched, speechless, as both cars braked hard; both drivers looked briefly at each other; then the Mercedes moved off, its driver inscrutable behind a huge pair of sunglasses and a pink silk scarf, leaving Mrs Starr looking bashfully at Sam. She might even be blushing, Sam thought, since she prided herself on her driving, on never doing any of the silly things that women drivers were supposed (by men) to do.

'Don't you tell Dad,' she hissed.

Sam couldn't help smiling. She was relieved that her mother's sense of humour hadn't entirely vanished.

'I don't know, Mum. It doesn't seem to be your day.'

'You get going, Sam.' And the station wagon roared off towards the car park.

Sam turned towards the dinghy lockers, feeling that slightly guilty sense of triumph she had whenever her mother slipped up somewhere. As she herself admitted, her mother was tough on Dad and tough on the rest of them but she did silly things too, occasionally. Everyone did.

With difficulty, she and Jane managed to pull the dinghy from the locker but it was too heavy for them to lift and carry to the top of the ramp.

'Lift, Jane. Try harder,' grunted Sam.

'I can't. And you're only just getting it off the ground yourself. We'll have to wait until Mum comes. You know Dad'll go berko if we scratch his precious varnish on the concrete.' They stood by the dinghy, conscious of the hearty male voices echoing around the locker building.

'I wish Terry was here,' said Sam finally. 'You'd think some of those men might help us.'

'I'm glad they're not. We'll manage. Anyway, here's Mum.'

'I've had to wake Jeremy up,' said Mrs Starr as she approached. 'He's grumpy, so please take him gently, you two. Now, both of you get on the same side. I can manage the other. One, two, six.'

Even for the three of them it was a struggle to get the heavy clinker-built dinghy over the concrete. Gasping, they lowered it thankfully at the top of the wooden ramp. Sam took the painter and held the boat steady as it slid down towards the water, gathering speed as it went. An oily layer of green algae covered the ramp below the high-water mark, making it more slippery than an ice-skating rink. They had to tread cautiously on the low slats of wood that made a stairway up each side.

'Golly, Mum, look at Jeremy,' said Sam, seeing her young brother perched miserably on top of the life-jackets, clutching the packet of fish and chips to his chest like a hot-water bottle. 'What's all that blood on his shirt, and his hair?'

'I told you, he cut his head,' said Jane, picking up her bag. 'Scalps always bleed a lot.'

'He looks like a stretcher case.' She lowered her voice. 'Mum, couldn't he take off his shirt? Everyone's looking at him.'

Mrs Starr was already going down the ramp with the heavy plastic chilly bin in one hand, balanced by two sailing bags in the other. 'Sorry, Sam. I've more important things to worry about. Come on, Jeremy, you can take your bag. You're not that incapable.'

'It's not my fault,' protested Jeremy irritably. 'I couldn't help it if my head got cut open.'

'Well, you could take off your shirt,' said Sam.

'No. Get lost.'

'And look at your hair. It's all clotted up with blood. It looks awful.'

'Leave me alone, will you?'

There were only two sailing bags left. Sam took hers, and pointedly left the other for Jeremy.

'I can't take it,' he wailed, standing up with both arms clasped firmly around the fish and chips.

'I see. How handy,' muttered Sam. Close by walked an elderly yachtsman in white shorts, a skipperish sort of hat and brand new navy sandshoes, audibly sharing his opinion that 'noisy children should be left at home with their mothers . . . can't take the noise of children arguing . . .' Mrs Starr heard this too as she came panting up the ramp. She briefly favoured the old die-hard with a sweet smile.

'Come on, you two, we're winning,' she said, returning Sam's grin so that she knew they were both remembering their talk at breakfast. A little ashamed of herself, Sam picked up the two bags and followed Jeremy down the ramp. Jane was already sitting in the stern, her life-jacket on, watching Sam come down – no doubt, Sam thought, hoping I'll slip, little beast.

'Life-jacket, Jeremy. You get in the stern. Sam in the bow,' said Mrs Starr tersely, loading the last bags on top of the children's knees, and carefully passing over the packet of fish and chips for Sam to hold.

'What about Terry, Mum?' said Sam. She looked at her watch. 'It's ten to five. Do you think he'll come now?'

'He must. Though it's not like him to be late.' She was obviously reluctant to leave.

'Why don't we wait for Dad?' asked Sam. They all looked up at the loading bay area; there was less activity there now. Most of the competing yachts had left the marina and the women had driven off home in their cars. 'He said he'd be here shortly after five.'

Mrs Starr hesitated. 'No, that would be ten minutes wasted. We'll go out, then you can row back, Sam, and get him. Terry too, I hope. He must have been held up somewhere.' Mrs Starr carefully took her place amidships and steadied the oars as the dinghy drifted away from the ramp.

But they couldn't go quite yet. A car pulled up at the loading area with a squeal of brakes. That might be Terry. No – a harrassed youngish women dashed over to the gateway to the marina berths carrying a flat parcel. She stopped and stared. The Starr family watched in amazement. After a brief, tense pause, she looked around and her eyes lit on the little dinghy just pulling away from the ramp. 'Here, wait,' she cried. 'You take it.'

'Take what?' said Sam to her mother.

The woman came teetering down the ramp, obviously upset. 'That is the last time I spend all Friday preparing food for my husband to take on the boat. Here, you have it. You'll enjoy it more than a bunch of ungrateful men, and my kids won't eat it.'

She thrust out the parcel – food of some sort.

'It's a pavlova. I left it behind on the kitchen bench, and I've just driven all the way home to get it. They couldn't wait even ten minutes. Never again. *Never.*'

'Couldn't we try to find the boat and hand it over tomorrow?' asked Mrs Starr.

'No. They don't deserve it, and it wouldn't keep in this heat.' Up from the car came the wail of a baby, and Sam now saw three small children, none older than six or seven, staring down from the top of the ramp.

'You're very kind,' said Mrs Starr warmly. 'What's your husband's boat? If we see him during the weekend we'll tell him you tried.'

'Division Three. The boat's called *Allegro*. His name's Russell. Right at this moment I wish the boat would sink with all hands. Without trace,' she added with relish.

'We'll enjoy the pavlova for tea,' said Sam. 'We're going on the race too, if we make it in time. Mum burnt our bacon and egg pie today and nearly set the house on fire.'

'A slight exaggeration, Sam,' began Mrs Starr, but the woman had turned around and was laughing. For a moment Sam wondered whether she should have volunteered that information about the pie – then with relief heard her mother laughing too.

'Well, we all have our problems,' said the woman, shooing her children before her back up the ramp. 'Yours are going sailing, mine are staying at home.'

'You've certainly got a handful there. Thanks again,' called Mrs Starr.

Once more Sam pushed the dinghy away from the ramp and they began the long row out to *Aratika*. The pavlova lady was already shutting the car doors firmly on her brood of small children.

'What a *handful*!' said Mrs Starr, looking up at the departing car as she settled into a steady rowing rhythm. Her back was towards Sam, but there was no mistaking the sympathy in her voice.

CHAPTER 5

Dad, but no Terry

The row out to *Aratika* through the great fleet of moored boats never failed to delight Sam; it was a promise of pleasures ahead and a quiet interlude between the bustle of activity at the ramp and the work of preparing the yacht for sea.

Today, sitting in the bow of the dinghy facing for'ard with the steaming newspaper packet of fish and chips across her knees and, above that, the flat shape of the pavlova parcel, her sense of anticipation was keener than usual. It wasn't, she decided, just the fact that they were going on a race, with the added tension of running late; something else was contributing to her excitement. There must be something special about sailing at night, as Dad had said this morning.

Behind her, she could hear the creak of the brass rowlocks and the fast splash of the oars. 'That way, Mum,' and 'Left hand down a bit,' came from Jeremy and Jane in the stern, directing the little dinghy past the buoys and anchor warps and motionless hulls.

They were certainly shifting, thought Sam, looking down at the bow waves rippling outwards, even with the weight of four passengers and all the gear. The tide was against them too. Over to their left in the fairway, keelers were still making their way towards the gap in the breakwater, their crews busy on deck bending on sails and hoisting racing pennants.

After six or seven minutes of hard rowing the familiar shape of *Aratika* drew nearer, sometimes visible, sometimes hidden by other boats. At last they came into the small area of open water which surrounded her. For

44

some reason, this final approach was one of Sam's most treasured moments in sailing; she gazed with renewed awe at the sturdy varnished mast which seemed to reach to the sky, and at the paintwork shining smooth and white as ice. She ran her hand almost reverently along the slippery surface, fending off while her mother skilfully brought the dinghy alongside. No one spoke. The procedure was familiar. Jane climbed on board first, taking the painter, and Jeremy shifted his weight to counterbalance her. The gear went next, with Stormy in his box; then Jeremy. Sam handed up the pavlova and the fish and chips separately to Jane.

'Right, Sam, she's all yours. Mind where you go.' Mrs Starr swung herself up over the liferails. 'And hurry. Dad should be waiting by now, and Terry too, hopefully.'

She scanned the distant clubhouse area, but because of the forest of masts it was impossible to distinguish any figures waiting by the ramp. 'We can't go racing if he doesn't show up.'

Sam looked up dismayed. 'Oh, Mum. After all this? We can manage.'

'I'm not arguing about it now,' said Mrs Starr with finality. She began to loosen the dinghy painter, but hesitated before casting off. 'Jane, I think you'd better go too. You'll be able to help her see where she is going. I can manage here. Leave your life-jacket on.'

'Do I have to?' said Jane, without enthusiasm.

'Yes.'

Jane shrugged and climbed down into the bow of the dinghy.

'You'll have to sit in the stern, Jane,' cried Mrs Starr, exasperated. 'Watch what you're doing . . .' The dinghy rocked alarmingly as Jane clambered over the top of Sam.

'Mind out,' protested Sam.

'You'd be better rowing from the bow,' called Mrs Starr. She tossed the painter into the boat.

Sam, having repositioned the rowlocks and the oars with some difficulty, pulled uncertainly away. It always took her a minute or two to get her rhythm. A red-billed seagull, flawless white and grey, mocked her efforts from a nearby pile. 'Oink, oink,' mimicked Jane. 'Look, Sam, he's only got one leg.'

'The poor thing,' began Sam, but she was interrupted by a cry from *Aratika*: 'Sam, get going.'

Oh Mum, just for two seconds, let me look at a seagull! Sam pulled strongly at the oars. The dinghy, now going with the incoming tide and relieved of all the gear, responded so well that she had to alter course to avoid colliding with a small launch. Carefully not looking over at *Aratika* to see if her mother was still watching, she settled into a steady tempo, guided by Jane.

Boats were still proceeding down the fairway – enough of them to compel Sam to rest briefly on her oars and wait for a gap in the traffic. One great white monster swept dramatically past, her skipper giving a cheerful wave, the high curve of her topsides towering over the two girls. That was the biggest keeler on the harbour. And there was another First Division maxi-racer; if her skipper had seen the small dinghy waiting, he gave no sign. Sam's arms were aching, and like her mother earlier, she was panting. Then Jane gave a shout.

'There's Dad!' Sam looked around. Yes, there he was, waving for all he was worth. She felt strong again and pulled the last fifty metres into the ramp with long firm strokes.

'Hi, girls!' he was shouting, his briefcase and arms at all angles and his working clothes looking oddly out of place. Heading down the ramp, he forgot the green slime and slipped, but with a mighty effort regained his balance – only to start ski-ing towards the water. Sam and Jane, watching fascinated from the bottom of the ramp, waited for the outcome. Dad on his trouser seat would be worth a dollar a minute. Or Dad in the tide even! But it was too much to hope for. Mr Starr salvaged what little dignity remained with a do-or-die stride straight into the dinghy and collapsed with a grunt on the floorboards.

'Whoa, Dad,' gasped Jane, clutching her knees with mirth, while in the bow Sam was momentarily tangled up with the top half of a large body, several arms, a briefcase and two oars. The dinghy rocked and tilted crazily.

'Oh, Dad,' gulped Jane, 'that was close. You've no idea how funny that looked.' There was an ironic cheer from an onlooker above.

'Oh, yes I have,'grinned their father. 'Like a scarecrow on skates.' The dinghy gradually came to rest. Sam and Jane were laughing so much they completely forgot about the race and their anxious mother out in the yacht.

'Here, we'd better get going,' said Mr Starr. 'I'll row, Sam. I didn't drop my briefcase in all that flurry, did I?'

'No, it's here, Dad, on my lap.'

'Thank goodness for that. Lucky I didn't go straight through the floorboards. I'll have to get my shoes off. I can't row in *shoes*.' He pulled off his black city shoes, then reached back to move the rowlocks and oars amidships. 'How's Mum? And Terry?'

'That's the trouble,' said Sam, unpleasantly reminded of the implications of his absence. 'Terry hasn't turned up. We hoped he'd be waiting here with you.'

'Drat the boy. He said he'd be here at four. If I can get here on time on a bus, I daresay Terry ought to be able to manage it on his motorbike.'

'Something must have happened, Dad. He's never been late before,' said Sam loyally. 'Not once.'

'No. True. Well, let's get out to the boat anyway. Pass me those oars, Sam. We might have time to take a run in under motor and check. Then again,' he added, looking at his watch, 'we might not.'

47

'Mum says we won't be able to go in the race if he doesn't turn up,' said Jane. 'He won't come now, Dad.'

The answer was a mumbled 'We'll see.' Mr Starr braced his feet firmly before swinging into a long powerful stroke which carried the dinghy straight across the fairway and out into the thick of the moored boats in a few seconds. He made his way expertly through the fleet as though he had eyes in the back of his head.

Sam watched his broad back straining back and forth. She felt good. Dad was here, in charge: her Dad who knew everything there was to know about boats, and who would skipper them through the calm clear night to Kawau.

'Did I tell you it's just two days short of a full moon?' said Mr Starr suddenly. 'That'll make your Mum happy.' Five or six pulls on the oars later, he added, 'I hope.'

CHAPTER 6

Under way

Less than ten minutes later, the Starr family put to sea. Looking back on the events of that night, Sam was to wonder why it all seemed so inevitable; why no one in those tense hours leading up to the start of the race had cried 'Stop'. They could so easily have decided to forego the race and, as Mum had suggested earlier, just pottered off to some nearby anchorage for the night. The race would have waited until next year. Yet Sam knew that her mother had allowed herself to be overruled; in the end she did not want Dad to be disappointed and resentful. Family pressure, she decided, was a powerful thing.

As Sam had expected, the moment Dad stepped on board a sharp debate began about the advisability of going racing without an extra adult. Mum seemed tight-lipped and adamant, yet it was her gentle father who prevailed as he changed into his sailing gear. He agreed with her in principle, he said, but the weather surely justified a slight relaxation in the rules. 'Look at it,' he pleaded, waving vaguely at the cloudless sky.

Her mother just couldn't produce a counter-argument; it was, she said, bad seamanship to race short-handed. It didn't feel right. 'Intuition, if you like.'

'What does that mean, Mum?' asked Sam, as the whole family, except for Jeremy who was allowed to read below, helped to haul the heavy kauri dinghy on deck. 'One, two, six, *heave*,' called Dad.

'It's something women are supposed to have a lot of,' said her mother tartly. 'Funny feelings in your bones. A sixth sense that all is not as well as it seems.' The dinghy was finally in position behind the mast, over the top of the cabin.

Have I got intuition? thought Sam as she watched her father's strong hands, brown and roughened from their recent long cruise, firmly lashing the dinghy down. Or was it something that came, along with eyebrows and breasts and things, with changing from a girl into a woman? What could be Mum's 'intuition' about sailing to Kawau on a night like this? Funny feelings in your bones, indeed!

Dad was getting into his stride; the strange reversal of roles between her parents had already taken place. The decision to go had, it seemed, been made. 'Sam, ready to let go for'ard. Mum, take the tiller. I'll get her started and then Sam and I can get the main sail organized. Jane, keep out of the way.' He switched the diesel motor into life and strained at the heavy gear-lever low down under the cockpit seat. The engine was a comparatively recent addition to the boat and only Dad's arm was strong enough to work the lever. 'Now pull up on the mooring warp, Sam.'

Planting her feet on the foredeck, Sam hauled mightily on the thick, rough rope. Nothing happened at first, but, expecting this, Sam kept up the strain and gradually, very gradually, the pressure came off the loop around the bollard and she was able to lift it clear.

'Let go the buoy,' came her father's shout.

Slowly *Aratika* made way. Sam pushed the orange plastic buoy through the chrome stanchions of the pulpit and dropped it into the water. The pulpit and the wire liferails that formed a fence around the boat were William's only concession to modern yachting practice. Then she stood up and enjoyed the first breath of cooling breeze on her hot skin as the old yacht picked up speed and created its own wind. Leaning up against the forestay, she imagined herself as a figurehead on a sailing ship, sleek wooden curls streaming back, bosom held proudly above the waves. There was a figurehead in the

Auckland museum she always said hello to on school trips there.

'Come on, Sam. I need help with this sail.'

Sam made her way aft. A great crackling pile of white terylene suddenly appeared in the cockpit, half-smothering her mother at the tiller so that Mrs Starr had to stand up to see her way clear through the last of the moored boats before she reached open water. Yet there wasn't much Sam could do to help her father, other than hold the crisp material in bunches to prevent it flying away as his deft fingers swiftly inserted the battens into their pockets.

'Dad?' It was Jane's voice from the counter behind the cockpit where she had gone to keep out of the way. 'There's a big shiny orange boat coming up behind. It looks as though it wants to eat us up.'

'Can't look now.' He was intent on slotting the lower edge of the mainsail into the track along the boom. 'Tell it to go away.'

Sam turned to watch the sleek ten-metre boat draw slowly abreast. The hull was the colour of a ripe apricot and shiny as glass, the rigging silver, and the crew of seven or eight men leaning nonchalantly against the rigging were dressed in orange T-shirts and shorts. All men, of course, and not so young either – even Dad's age. A well-fed lot, she guessed, with those male figures that look slim from back and front but side on show a paunch being held in by tight shorts. She wondered, embarrassed by their close scrutiny, what they thought of Dad with his old boat and crew of wife and two girls. But Dad hadn't even stopped to look.

'*Aratika*? Division Five?'

Only then, his immediate task completed, did Mr Starr straighten up. 'That's us.'

'I've a message for you from Terry Andrews,' called the skipper, superb in white behind the wheel. 'He tried to let

51

you know he wouldn't be on board tonight. His father's been taken ill. He flew off to Tauranga this afternoon.'

Mr Starr nodded. 'Thanks. We wondered where he'd got to.'

'Are you racing to Kawau?'

'Yes, if we make it to the start on time.'

'Good luck!'

Even during this short exchange, the ketch was already pulling ahead as the two boats approached the eastern end of the breakwater and the harbour beyond.

'Poor Terry,' said Sam. 'I knew something had happened, Dad.' But her father was not allowing time off to sympathize, nor even to admire the fancy artwork on the stern of the departing ketch, her name hand-painted in many scrolls and curlicues.

'Right, Sam,' her father was saying. Sam reluctantly turned her attention to their own mainsail. 'Keep the slides going into the track as I hoist.' With his first vigorous heave on the halyard, the flapping pile of terylene should have started on its way aloft; simultaneously there came a shout from Mrs Starr at the wheel and a muttered oath from her father.

'Nick! You haven't shackled on.'

'Curses! Sam, catch that thing.' The small stainless steel shackle which should have been firmly attached to the head of the mainsail was swinging round on the loose wire half-way up the mast, describing crazy circles in the air. Sam dropped her bunch of sail and waited for the halyard to swing towards her, but it was too high for her to catch, even if she stood on top of the dinghy.

'I can't reach . . .,' she began, but her father, already realizing this, was beside her on the cabin top and stretched up to grab the shackle on its next arc.

'Got you.' He coupled the halyard up to the sail. 'Now. We'll try again.' With the sudden shifting of Mr Starr's weight, *Aratika* was lurching grumpily from side

52

to side, her bare mast shaking an irritable finger at the sky.

'Comes of doing things in a hurry,' said a voice from the cockpit.

'Nobody's perfect,' muttered Mr Starr as this time the sail rose smoothly up the mast. 'It could have been worse, eh, Sam?' He grinned. 'Lucky I didn't have to go aloft in the bosun's chair. That would have been the last straw for your mother.' He looked up, checking the tautness of the luff of the sail as he winched the wire halyard around the drum. 'Don't want it too tight today. In light airs, it's better slightly eased off. Mum, get that sail drawing. Wind's from the south-east, such as it is. We're on a tight reach.'

'I know we're on a tight reach,' said Mrs Starr, her voice heavy with sarcasm. She loosened off the mainsheet until the great sail quite suddenly ceased its flapping and smoothed out into a white curve. 'Funny, now. I would never have thought to look and check what all the boats ahead were doing.'

'Can't say anything right,' mumbled her father, as he coiled up the main halyard in best Bristol fashion. 'Sam, get the big jib out, will you? The big genoa. What's the time? Twenty to six? It's going to be close.'

Sam dropped down through the for'ard hatch and pushed the big blue sailbag up onto the foredeck. 'I can put the jib on, Dad,' she said eagerly. This was something she could do.

'Okay. I'll get the jib sheets.'

Carefully, for the deck was now heeling with the combined thrust of both the motor and mainsail together, she climbed out onto the sturdy wooden bowsprit and sat astride it. She leaned squarely against the pulpit so that she felt balanced and both her hands were free to pull the big sail towards her and hank it on to the forestay. First, the head onto the shackle and then the fiddly little bronze hanks. Finally, the shackle at the tack, and the sail bunched in folds at the foot of the forestay. A metre or so below her the water slipped gently past.

'Here are the jib sheets, Sam.' Her father seemed to be all over the boat at once, adjusting, checking, coiling up ropes, hoisting the burgee. He left the two thick coils of rope for her to shake out, and stood by to watch as she tied two cautious but perfect bowlines to secure the sheets to the clew of the sail.

'That's good, Sam.' He stood back to let her take the two sheets aft, one either side, through the fairleads on the deck and into the cockpit. She finished the job with a nice figure-of-eight knot at the end of each sheet.

'Good. Now do you want to hoist?'

'Okay.' She could manage this too, she knew, all except for the very last little bit when Dad's muscles were needed. Feeling confident, she went straight to the jib halyard, one of the many ropes at the foot of the mast, and hauled away. The genoa rose up the forestay. This time Mrs Starr anticipated the call and moved quickly to get the jib sheet around the winch. A few seconds of pulling, a few of winching and the sail was finally drawn in.

There was silence except for the chug of the engine; both yacht and crew seemed to be drawing breath, enjoying this first moment of answering to the breeze. Sam, standing on the foredeck, now noticed the throng of yachts ahead, so thick on the horizon that she could hardly believe her eyes. To the right, the busy port area slipped past: a familiar unfolding sequence of wharves, tankers, fishing boats, tugs and the ferry buildings; a great white passenger liner glowing in the sun; cranes, cargo ships of all shapes and sizes; the container terminal, always bustling, the red, white and blue containers stacked up like building blocks; Mechanics Bay and the amphibians lined up on the tarmac; the Compass Dolphin sitting round and squat by Hobson Bay; then the long wooden breakwater of Okahu Bay and another great fleet of boats moored inside. Sam loved this run from Westhaven to Orakei.

She shivered. Even though there was still plenty of heat in the sun, the breeze was making the hairs on her arms stand up, goose-pimpled. The cockpit would be more sheltered, she thought, so she slowly made her way aft and sat down close to her mother. For the first time since breakfast, the family was gathered together. At the tiller, Mum stared apprehensively at the yachts ahead. Dad squatted on the after deck behind her, his eyes running constantly over the boat in the manner, Sam had noticed, of all skippers: checking the rigging, the set of the sails, alert for any slight change in the wind and for the movement of other craft in the busy inner harbour. Sam saw that occasionally his eyes rested on her mother with an anxious, almost pleading expression. He seemed to be willing her to relax and enjoy the race.

Aratika drew abreast of the naval base on their left and a little further on passed the Devonport wharf where Dad caught his ferry to work each day. One was just leaving, a black and white steamboat, double-decked, with a tall smokestack amidships puffing a thin trail of smoke. Cars and people were lined up along the wharf, some to watch the start of the race and some, Sam knew, to fish for whitebait as she and Dad sometimes did, with huge home-made muslin nets, right under the 'No Fishing' sign.

'The tide's against us, I'm afraid,' said Mrs Starr, breaking the silence. 'High water at eight tonight, which means we'll have to be careful getting into Kawau through the passage. If it's a slow trip, the tide will be well on its way out. I can't see it being anything else but slow.'

They were approaching the outskirts of the race fleet. Over a hundred boats, William had said; to Sam's inexperienced eyes there seemed to be twice as many.

'We're on starboard, so we have right of way,' said Mr Starr.

'I wish you'd stop telling me things I already know,' Mrs Starr replied peevishly. 'Sam, you'd better sit down to leeward as lookout, please. I can't see under that great jib. Change places with Jane.'

'Can't I be lookout too?' objected Jane. 'I'm always being shoved out of the way and . . .'

'You can be lookout on the bowsprit, Jane,' Mr Starr put in quickly. 'We need all the lookouts we've got. Shout long and hard if you think there's any risk of collision.'

'Goody,' said Jane. She was always being told to keep her voice down. And the bowsprit was one of her favourite places, especially when a big sea was running and the bowsprit dipped deep into the troughs, then rose again like a finger pointing the way.

Sam, moving into the left side of the cockpit vacated by Jane, noticed that she was still shivering – not with cold now, but with excitement and nerves at the sight of all those yachts in a confined area, relentlessly jockeying for position.

'Are we really going to make it in time, Dad?' she asked.

'Ten to six. I think so. The Sixth Division should be going off now. Actually, there's a bit more breeze out here than one would think. We'll turn off the engine shortly.'

'Are you sure it's six, Nick?' asked Mrs Starr. 'Perhaps we'd better check the book.' Sam smiled. She knew Mum didn't have much confidence in her father's sense of time; for school, yes, he was very punctual, because he had to be, but not with family comings and goings, where he always seemed to be running ten minutes late. 'Would you get the book out of the shelf just inside the hatch, Sam?' asked her mother.

Sam handed her father the slim blue booklet containing

the racing instructions, courses and the start times for the whole season. 'Here we are, Mum,' he said, finding the page swiftly. 'Night Passage Race to Kawau. Division Five . . . eighteen zero-five hours. Eighteen zero-*five*?' He looked sheepish. 'Just as well we checked. We've got an extra five minutes.'

'Just as well, he says! Honestly, Nick . . .'

'How far is the race, Dad?' Sam interrupted.

He went gratefully back to the book. 'Distance forty-one kilometres. Safety regulations, page twenty-five. I know one thing we've forgotten – the racing pennant. I put it on board last weekend. Have you seen it in your travels, Mum?'

'Port locker. What are they?'

'What are what?'

'The safety regulations, see page twenty-five.'

'Oh, those. Well, briefly, I'll tell you. Minimum equipment – life-jackets for each person on board. Naturally. One lifebuoy, preferably orange – yes. Flares – yes. Safety harness for each crew working for'ard – yes. Dinghy carried on deck – yes. Fire extinguishers and first aid kit – of course. Hand bilge pump – yes. Bucket – yes. Navigation lights, compass and chart. Two anchors. Spare tiller. Yes, yes, yes. I checked them all over last weekend.'

He snapped the book shut, dropped below, and reappeared with the purple racing pennant, which he fixed to the backstay.

'Now, Mum, I'll take the tiller. We can get that engine off. Anything we've forgotten to do before we join the dance? You've stowed everything away?'

Mrs Starr, deep in her own thoughts, nodded vaguely. She handed over the tiller and stood by the open hatchway. About a hundred metres ahead the outer boats of the great throng crossed and recrossed tacks, no two boats on the same course.

'Switch off the engine, Mum,' said the skipper, his voice tense.

The sudden silence seemed to wrap itself around Sam like a soft shawl, and the irritation that a spell under motor always built up inside her disappeared. She gave a long sigh of relief.

Jeremy's voice came up from the depths of the cabin.

'Aaah – that's better,' he cried in an old man's quavery voice. They all laughed, even Mum.

Small sounds could be heard: the gentle hiss of the bow wave foaming past the cockpit, the cheep-cheep of the slender kawhai bird overhead, the creak of the mast. Even Stormy, who had disappeared into some dark corner the moment he had been let out of his box, now judged it safe to reappear on deck, picking his way carefully through the ropes on the cockpit floor before leaping up lightly onto Sam's bare knees. His claws pricked her briefly, then he settled into his sphinx position, his grey fur warm against her skin.

'Keep your eyes peeled, Sam,' warned her father. 'And when we start tacking you'll have to put that cat down.'

The race was on.

CHAPTER 7

A spinnaker start

Like a leaf to a whirlpool in a mountain stream, *Aratika* was being drawn into the circling assembly of yachts now concentrated in a half-kilometre area west of the wharf which jutted out from the far end of the breakwater. It was the job of each skipper to manoeuvre his boat into a good position, so that when his division's gun was fired, he was just short of the line between the starter's box and a red marker buoy about two hundred metres distant; but he should not be across that invisible line, not even by the tip of a bowsprit, before the gun.

It was also the skipper's job to avoid collisions and to give way if he was on port tack. Sam was glad that her father was an old hand at this. She wasn't too sure which would be worse: a good wind which would at least allow a boat to be swung quickly onto a new tack, or this gentle breeze which meant that it took longer for a yacht to answer the helm – more, she remembered Dad once saying, in the style of the old sailing ships.

Skippers claimed right of way with harsh, urgent shouts of 'Staaaarboard,' causing boats on port tack to spin away, their crews heaving on the sheets, winches singing and the sails flapping noisily in protest. Sam knew that such a big start looked a shambles from shore; to be in the thick of it was, she decided, no less of a shambles.

'Yellow boat to port,' called Sam.

'Green one in front,' yelled Jane.

'Navy ketch coming up fast to port,' warned Mrs Starr.

'Starboard,' shouted Mr Starr with glee. He held *Aratika* to her course. He might have to take avoiding action, even yet. At the last possible moment, it seemed to

Sam, the skipper of the navy ketch tacked away, followed by four other boats on port, while the green boat ahead also altered her course away from them all. Sam laughed. What a path they had cut! Her father was grinning too. Even Jeremy couldn't resist coming on deck to watch the action.

There was a muffled bang from the direction of the wharf.

'Was that a gun, Dad?' asked Sam.

He looked at his watch.

'Yes, five to six exactly. That's Division Six going off, and our ten minute gun.'

Sam could now pick out a pattern from the confusion: the smallest keelers in the fleet had shaken themselves clear from the crowd and were heading purposefully in a group towards the line. Spinnakers of every colour appeared like magic.

'Oh, look. Look!' cried Jane from the bowsprit.

'You look for collisions, Jane,' warned her father. 'We'll have to go about shortly, and we'll be on port tack.' *Aratika* was getting close to the breakwater. 'Put the cat down, Sam. Ready with the jib sheets. I'll do the backstays. Ready about. Lee-oh.'

He pushed the tiller hard over; the boom swung across while Sam let go one jib sheet and her mother swiftly pulled in the other, cranking the rope home on the winch until the jib was drawn into a tight curve. Now they themselves were obliged to give way to any boat on starboard.

Sam was trembling with excitement. The warm patch where Stormy had been sitting felt cold and bare. She looked around for him, but he was nowhere to be seen.

'Where's Stormy?'

'For crying out loud, Sam, don't ask me to look for the cat now,' said her father. The breakwater was a little closer than was comfortable in the light breeze.

'Orange boat coming up to starboard,' called Mrs Starr. 'You haven't seen it, have you, Nick!'

From her father's swift reaction, Sam could tell that indeed he had not seen that orange boat hidden in the blind spot behind the low curtain of the jib. Again Mum was one jump ahead. Instead of tacking, he decided to alter course slightly, to go under the stern of the orange boat so that she crossed ahead of *Aratika* by a few metres.

'Thanks, Mum. Any others I can't see?'

'Yes, several, in half a minute or so.'

'Right. We'll run off. Loosen the jib sheets.' Now *Aratika* was running before the wind, right away from the press of yachts. 'We'll do one gybe in a couple of minutes, and then run back on starboard to the line.'

Once more he checked his watch, then made a careful survey of their position in relation to the fleet.

'Four minutes to go. Oh, boy. There's trouble.' He pointed over towards North Head, where a huge container ship, red, square and ugly, was coming round the channel buoys into harbour.

'Do they have to bring ships into the harbour right in the middle of a race?' asked Sam. 'Couldn't they wait for a bit?'

'I can't imagine that the harbourmaster would be too sympathetic to that suggestion,' said her father, laughing. 'Holding up overseas ships for a lot of pleasure boats? We're very dependent on our imports in this country, you know,' he added in his schoolmaster's voice.

In case any crews had not yet seen the menacing wall of scarlet steel now swinging round North Head, the heavily-laden ship gave five clear hoots which rang round the harbour and echoed faintly from the city's hills.

'What's that, Dad?' asked Jeremy, struggling with a petrified Stormy. The cat squirmed his way out of his arms and vanished below.

'That means he wants to make double sure we've all

seen him. It means I can't get out of your way, so you get out of mine!'

'But I thought power always gave way to sail.'

'As a general rule, yes. But not if it's a great big ship like that coming up a narrow channel. It's our responsibility to keep out of his way then.'

'Big bully,' said Jeremy. Sam also felt intimidated by that massive steel wall sliding remorselessly through the water. High above, on the flying bridge, she could see tiny figures, and higher still, flags of red, white and yellow.

There was a sudden roar ahead, completely obliterating all other sounds.

'Honestly, this harbour is like Piccadilly Circus,' said her mother. They all watched fascinated as an amphibian taking off from Mechanics Bay skidded under the thrust of full power across the smooth water.

'It's going awfully close to those boats,' pointed Sam as the small aircraft, making a noise out of all proportion to its size, seemed to head straight for a cluster of First Division boats which, being the last to start for Kawau, were keeping aloof from the smaller boats. Finally the pilot persuaded his machine clear of the water and slowly gained height, seeming to thread his way among the tall masts.

'I wouldn't like to have been on those boats,' said Sam, impressed.

'It wasn't nearly as close as it looked, Sam,' smiled her father. 'Probably on its way to Kawau, twenty minutes flying time. I'd rather be down here.' To the family's astonishment, he broke into song:

> 'I am sailing – I am *sailing*
> Home again – 'cross the sea –
> I am sailing – stormy waters . . .'

and equally abruptly, broke off. 'Right. We've had the

curtain-raisers. Two minutes to go. We'll run back for the line now. Maximum concentration, please, from everybody. You okay, Jane?' he called forward. 'We're going to run for the line now.'

'Yep,' replied Jane.

Sam winched in the jib sheet as her father gradually brought *Aratika* onto a reach and back towards the congested starting area.

'Nick, you're going to be too early!' There was exasperation in her mother's voice.

'I don't think so. Pull in the jib sheet a bit, Sam. If we come on the wind we'll slow down a bit.'

Mrs Starr, not giving Sam time to react, leapt across the cockpit and attacked the winch. Annoyed, Sam looked away and tried to make herself useful by finding the red buoy which marked the outer limit of the starting line. She hated being pushed aside. But through the thick forest of masts and sails she could see nothing. Again, *Aratika* on starboard cut a path through the crowd as she slowly neared the start area.

Just as Mum had said at breakfast, nearly all the crews were men. In fact there was only one other family that Sam could see, with a boy of about eight and two preschoolers firmly tied into life-jackets. Some yachts had the elderly owner's elderly wife sitting primly in the cockpit; others were crewed by young couples, with the men doing the sailing and their bikini-clad mates draped idly across the foredeck, only permitted to be mere passengers. Then she noted a slim girl on a boat about the same size as *Aratika*. In a pale blue bikini, she appeared to be efficiently readying the spinnaker gear all by herself. Now that, thought Sam, watching with admiration as the yacht sailed parallel to *Aratika*, is what I'd like to look like in five years' time.

'Sam, stop gawking and let out that jib sheet. We're reaching again.' Her father was slowly easing *Aratika* around so that she was pointing straight at the starting box perched on the end of the wharf, signal flags flying, maybe fifty metres away. The race officials up there were preparing to fire off the gun and hoist the Fifth Division's flag.

'One minute,' Sam heard a nearby skipper call. He was flying a purple flag too.

Mr Starr held *Aratika* on her course for another twenty seconds, bringing her so close to the wharf that he could have thrown a rope to the spectators. Sam watched, fascinated; the whole family seemed to be holding its breath, waiting for Dad to put the boat off the wind and make his final run for the line.

'Round we go!' He put the helm over, letting out the mainsheet with a rattle so that the heavy boom swung out wide and free. Sam eased the genoa sheet through the winch to loosen the jib into a full billowing arc. Now *Aratika* was set fair for the line, and all the Fifth Division boats, maybe twenty of them, were making their run.

This was the most decisive moment of the race. It needed only a small error of judgement on the part of the skipper and *Aratika* would arrive at the starting line just a fraction of a second too early.

'Ten seconds.' If Dad had misjudged his run, they would have to go back and cross the line again; no easy or quick manoeuvre through a hundred boats. Sam was trembling with tension.

Slowly the assembled division moved towards the line. *Aratika* was well placed among the first group of six or seven boats, lined up like knights on horseback, purple pennants flying from the rigging, their sails eased and full before the wind.

'Charge,' shouted Sam.

'Three . . . two . . . one . . .' Dad counted off on his watch.

Bang! And 'whooooooooooooo' followed immediately

on a hooter. They all looked across at the starting box in time to see the wisp of smoke from the gun curling upwards.

'What's *that*?' exclaimed Jeremy.

'The first boat must have been over the line,' said Dad grinning. 'Ha – it's old Wally. Bad luck, mate.'

'You got a great start, Dad,' said Sam.

'About eight metres short! Not bad, not bad at all,' he said. 'Poor old Wally. I don't envy him having to take a turn through that lot behind.' They saw Wally had already gybed away from their division, back into the crowd.

'Poor things,' said Sam sympathetically.

'Oh – it can happen to the best of them, even Wally, who's one of the best skippers around. One of William's vintage. Been sailing round this harbour for fifty years or more.'

Sam felt the tension evaporate. The big red ship had passed behind the Sixth Division fleet and was now well on her way up the harbour. There was clear water ahead, and the risk of collision was over. North lay Tiri passage and Kawau. But now she held her breath as one after another there were silent explosions of brilliant colour at the masts of all their rivals. Puff – there bloomed a spinnaker of scarlet and gold, like a sunset. Whoosh – another, several shades of emerald and kingfisher, deep ocean colours. Over there, look! – turquoise and lime green. Others of rainbow stripes, wasp stripes, barber pole stripes, diagonals and stars, circles and moons. Plain violet, icy blue, superb yellow, proud purples and browns. Even, amidst all the colours of the paintbox, a spinnaker of dignified pure white.

Sam gazed in wonder. She had never seen anything so beautiful. The spinnakers unfolded around her like fireworks. Most of the fleet were astern of *Aratika* so that the late afternoon sun behind them shone through each spinnaker as it unfurled while the south-easterly swung them gently from side to side. She climbed out onto the after deck to get a clearer view. It was only after a minute or two that she became conscious of voices, mostly Jane's.

'. . . please, Dad? Just the little one. We're the only boat not flying a spinnaker. Oh *please*, Dad. The little turquoise terror? We hardly ever get a chance to see the spinnaker up.'

Sam didn't turn around. She could see Dad in her mind's eye, pulling thoughtfully at the tiller, squinting at the clouds, and appraising the other spinnakers, the wind, the hours left before sunset. He wouldn't be hurried. Under her biggest jib and full main *Aratika* was certainly slipping along nicely, but already the extra sails on her competitors were beginning to tell. As the bunch of yachts approached the steep green slope of North Head, Sam counted that they had dropped back from second boat to about seventh. Yet the idea of putting up the small spinnaker – any spinnaker – worried her. On the rare occasions when Dad had decided to put one up with the family on board, it was always with a great deal of fuss and noise, he and Terry leaping madly around the boat and Mum watchful and nervous at the helm. She listened for Dad's reply, half hoping he would say no, but half hoping they could be in the race properly.

'What do you think, Mum?' he said at length. 'I feel we could manage the small one comfortably until sunset. I'd like to see how we go under these conditions, and it's a good opportunity for Sam to help me. What do you feel?'

No use asking Mum, thought Sam. She's sure to say no, with all that carry-on earlier about intuition. She watched with interest as a nearby boat, flying a very large red and black spinnaker, lost a vital rope and the wind at the same time. The spinnaker collapsed, the pole dropped, the skipper jumped up and down, the crew did frantic things on the foredeck. She turned round to see Mum and Dad watching too, both amused. Other people's spinnaker troubles always looked a riot – until you had one of your own. Surprisingly, Mum had not yet pronounced on their own spinnaker, for or against. There was no accounting for mothers. This one looked relaxed, and seemed to be enjoying herself.

'Well, what do you think, Mum?'

'*Please*, Mum,' put in Jane. 'Look, all the other boats are beating us now.'

Mrs Starr was also gazing thoughtfully around, seeing how the other boats were carrying their kites. Apart from the red and black job still hanging in folds by the mast and the skipper purple with rage, no one was having any problems.

'Over to you, Nick.' That meant, Sam and Jane knew, that while she still mightn't fully agree, she wasn't going to oppose the decision.

'Good-o,' said Dad.

'Hurray,' cried Jane. Sam didn't contribute to the general acclaim from her perch on the after deck. Some of her mother's earlier uneasiness seemed to have rubbed off on her. Spinnakers, although nice to look at, gave her the creeps.

'Right!' Mr Starr became brisk and bossy again. 'Mum, you take the tiller. Sam, get the spinnaker sheets and foreguy out of the after locker. Mum will show you which ones. Jeremy, stay right there.' A quite unnecessary direction as Jeremy was once again reclining on a bunk below, his nose in a book and Stormy on his tummy, both totally uninterested in anything that went on above. 'Sam, on your feet.'

Mr Starr stood up in the cockpit and gave a great stretch, while Sam slowly made her way for'ard with the sheets.

'You should have a life-jacket on, Sam,' called Mrs Starr. 'Here catch.'

Horrible bulky thing, thought Sam, as she reluctantly pulled the orange jacket over her head, but she knew better than to object. Family rules were family rules; and this was one of the strictest. All Children To Wear Life-Jackets While Working Under Way On Deck. Dad had even written it out in an official-looking notice and sellotaped it near the hatchway. He hadn't been in the Navy for nothing.

'Look, there's William,' suddenly shouted Jane, waving furiously. Sam and her father were stopped in their tracks. They gazed up at the crest of North Head, now abeam and only about a hundred metres from them.

'My word, Jane, I'm surprised you could pick him up with your eyes,' said Mrs Starr also waving. 'Did you know he was going to be there?'

'No, but it is him, isn't it?'

'Looks like him. Have a look through the binoculars, Jane,' said Mr Starr. The family waved madly and the small figure of an old man, bow-legged in baggy shorts, responded.

'Only William wears shorts like those! How he'd love to be coming too,' said Mrs Starr.

'That's what he said this morning,' said Sam. 'Then he said he was too old for racing. It must be awful knowing you're too old.'

'Yes.' Her father had stopped waving and was leaning against the shrouds. 'But memories have their own satisfaction. He'll be sitting up there remembering all the night races he did, as if he were running through his own private film show.'

'*He'd* like to see the spinnaker up, wouldn't he, Dad,' said Jane.

'Yes, indeed. Sam, you unlash the spinnaker pole. I'll get the sailbag.' He disappeared through the for'ard hatch, reappearing almost immediately with the red nylon bag containing the smaller of the two spinnakers.

Together they went through the procedure: shackle on the halyard, ready the spinnaker pole out to the starboard side, hitch on the sheet and guy, the two ropes leading back into the cockpit by which the spinnaker would be controlled. Sam's fingers were cold. Once she slipped, landing heavily on her thigh. If her mother noticed this, she made no sympathetic noises from the helm. Sam, tears springing to her eyes, knew that a hurt had to be considerable before Mum got concerned. One thing her mother didn't fuss over – small bumps and bruises.

'You all right, Sam?' asked her father, putting his hand on her shoulder. She nodded. It was strange; Dad was the softie in her family, Mum the battling soldier who never cried.

'Okay, then. We're ready to hoist. Would you like to do it?'

As Sam pulled on the halyard, the flimsy sail slithered upwards out of its bag until it hung in folds by the mast. She carefully coiled the rope around the wooden cleat on the mast, conscious of her father watching. A half-hitch would secure it.

'Good girl.'

Then together they clipped on the heavy varnished spinnaker pole, which would hold the big sail clear of the boat.

'Bring in that spinnaker guy, Mum,' he yelled.

As she did so, the south-easterly caught the sail, filling it abruptly into a half-balloon of pale glistening turquoise. *Aratika* was now taking her proper place in the fleet. Sam hoped that William had been watching them.

'Well done, both,' called her mother warmly from the cockpit, which was praise indeed – undoubtedly for getting the kite up without a lot of fuss and bother. With the foredeck cleared of loose rope ends and the big jib dropped temporarily to give the spinnaker maximum free air, they returned to the cockpit and her father settled down to the aspect of sailing he enjoyed most: trimming the sails. In a bit, out a bit, bring the spinnaker pole back a bit, try the mainsail in a touch, Mum: sailing for its own sake.

'I do hope William has noticed,' said Sam, looking back at North Head.

'Bound to, with those great binoculars of his,' said Mr Starr, not taking his eyes off the spinnaker. 'He'll be waiting for the big boats in the First Division. They'll all have their biggest kites up, shooters, the lot. It'll be a brave sight from North Head.'

'That's a brave sight too,' said Mrs Starr, her eyes following the gentle swaying movement aloft. 'Just the right amount of breeze to be comfortable.'

'Yes, this is your sort of weather, isn't it?' teased Mr Starr.

'And why not? We're not all masochists. Why should it be considered somehow superior to say you actually like Force 8 gales and hanging on by your fingernails? It's a male pose, half the time.'

'William told me this morning that grandmother used to like the lee rails under, the more wind the better,' said Sam.

'Did she now! Well, I'm different. And she was different from most women I've talked to. Nearly all of them say they hate it when it gets really rough.'

'Why?' put in Jane from behind the binoculars. 'Are they afraid their husbands will fall overboard?'

Her contribution to the conversation, although meant to be a joke, killed it stone dead. Sam saw her mother's expression close up with that blank look again. You idiot, Jane, she thought; Mum was just beginning to relax. She had touched a sore spot. Isn't falling overboard every sailor's unspoken fear?

Mr Starr broke the silence. 'We'll carry the spinnaker until about ten minutes before sundown. Best not to be taking it down in the dark, short-handed as we are.'

Her mother nodded, still preoccupied with her own thoughts. Sam again looked back at North Head. Among the division *Aratika* was now about half-way back, but keeping pace as far as she could tell since the boats were beginning to spread out across Rangitoto Channel. Over to the left, about a kilometre away, the smooth sweep of Cheltenham Beach ran like a tawny ribbon from the rocky base of North Head. She knew she could pick out William's place if she looked hard, but not their own house which stood back from the beach.

'I do hope William has seen the spinnaker,' she said again.

'I do hope it's time for tea,' said a bored voice from the cabin. 'I'm starved.' It was Jeremy; like Jane, always thinking of his stomach, thought Sam. But she realized suddenly that she was very hungry, too!

CHAPTER 8

Tea time

'Half past six,' Dad said. 'Time for fish and chips.'

No wonder Sam was famished. Only a biscuit to eat after school in all that hassle of burnt pie and the rush to get out of the house.

'I'll get them,' she said eagerly, swinging herself down into the cabin, but Jeremy was already unwrapping the huge parcel on the chart table and the delicious smell made her mouth water. She watched him carefully while she got out the plastic plates to make sure he didn't sneak any extra chips.

'Ah . . . smell *that*,' said Jeremy as he peeled back the last layer of newspaper with the air of a magician producing a rabbit out of a hat. Sam spread the five plates around the outside of the glistening pile of chips. Together they dug deep to find the pieces of fish.

'Two for me. Two for you. Two for Jane. Two for Mum. Three for Dad.' Jeremy's hand had become a front-end loader scooping up chips. 'A pile of chips for me. A pile for you. A pile for Jane. A smaller pile for Mum. The biggest pile for Dad. They're not very hot, are they?'

'You've given yourself more than me or Jane,' objected Sam. 'Here, take some off.'

'No, I haven't.' But he slid four chips onto Jane's plate and four onto Sam's. 'Happy now, fusspot?'

'Would you pass up two cans of beer, Sam?' came Dad's voice from the cockpit.

'And there's some made-up orange drink in the chilly bin,' added Mum. 'Pass up the whole container. I'll pour it up here. Be careful with those plates, Jeremy . . .' Her

72

voice rose as Jeremy thrust two loaded plates up towards the cockpit.

Sam found the beer cans and the orange drink; she couldn't resist cramming a handful of chips into her mouth before she organized the glasses. Then she climbed out into the cockpit with her plate and settled down to serious eating.

'What about some tomato sauce?' said Jeremy.

'You're already half-way through your chips,' said Jane pointedly.

'I'd still like some tomato sauce. You're nearest, Sam.'

Sam, her mouth full of fish, looked resentful and turned to her mother for support, but before she could say anything Mrs Starr said apologetically, 'Please, Sam? It would be less general schemozzle for everyone.'

'Oh yes, but not for me. Oh – okay!' She took another big mouthful of chips; she would make Jeremy wait half a minute at least. Finally, just before she sensed her mother was about to ask again, she put down her half-empty plate and went below for the tomato sauce.

'Not so much, Jeremy.' Mr Starr watched in horror as Jeremy upended the plastic bottle over his plate. 'Here, give me some.' Sam smiled. Dad had a thing about tomato sauce.

'That's better,' said Jane with relish, licking her fingers, then wiping them on her shorts. 'Now can we have some of that pavlova?'

'What pavlova?' said Mr Starr. 'You've never brought a pav on the boat, Mum. Not very suitable as boat nosh, I would have thought.'

'I agree. All that cream! No, I didn't make it. Just before we left the ramp at Westhaven a woman came roaring up in her car. The poor thing had been all the way home to get it – and then she found her husband's boat hadn't waited, even though it was one of the bigger boats and started later than us.'

'So she gave it to us,' said Jane. 'She was real mad.'

Mr Starr laughed. 'I'm not surprised. What boat was it?'

'Something like allergy.'

'No, you twit. "Allegro". It's Italian for fast,' Sam said, remembering music lessons at school. 'A nice name for a boat, I think.'

'Well, I don't,' said Jane. 'Anyway, there's a whacking great pavlova sitting in the sink. It's the only place we could find to put it. Can we *have* some?' she pleaded.

Mrs Starr looked doubtful. 'Pavlova on top of fish and chips?'

'Could we keep it until tomorrow?' said Mr Starr, putting down his beer can to adjust the spinnaker sheet.

'Mmm – it's not a good idea to keep cream overnight without a fridge,' said Mrs Starr. 'Obviously the boat it was intended for had one.'

'Quite a lot do, these days. Still, we get by, keeping things simple,' said Mr Starr, draining his can, his voice just a shade smug.

'Mum, can we have some pavlova, please?' persisted Jane.

'Later on, Jane. Give your fish and chips a chance to settle first. Sam hasn't even finished hers yet.'

Her initial hunger satisfied, Sam was quietly enjoying each of her remaining chips. That shop had the best chips in Auckland: long, crisp and salty. 'These are better than burnt pie,' she gently teased her mother.

'What burnt pie? Something else I haven't heard about,' said her father quickly.

Oh, hell! Perhaps Mum hadn't wanted to tell him. Embarrassed, she busied herself licking her fingers, waiting for her mother's reaction, and was relieved when her mother went on to explain about the call from school and the forgotten pie. There was even some praise for the way Sam had turned off the oven at the main switch and carried the pie outside. Typical of adults. No thanks or bouquets at the time, when she most needed to be told she'd done the right thing.

'Well done, Sam,' said her father. 'Perhaps we should put a bit of money aside and save up for a freezer for your Mum.'

'What help would a freezer be?' said Jeremy.

'Some people cook a whole lot of pies at once, and stick them in the freezer.'

'I wouldn't like to eat a frozen pie. Yuk.'

'You thaw it out, thicko,' said Jane.

'They're a lot of money for a little convenience, Nick,' Mrs Starr was saying. 'Normally, I can manage. Today, I don't know . . . what with Jeremy's cut . . .'

'Well,' Mr Starr replied heartily, 'we're here now. Your cut isn't bothering you, is it, Jeremy?'

'Nope,' said Jeremy, his attention on his orange drink. 'But it hurts when I frown, like this.'

'Don't do it then,' said Jane unsympathetically. 'You're just stretching the skin around the cut. You'll make it bleed again. Do you want to make it bleed again?'

'Let's have a look, lad,' said Mr Starr. He peered into the matted hair. 'It's not so bad, if you ignore all that dried blood.'

'The doctor said to clean it with Dettol and cut away the hair,' said Jeremy indignantly.

'That probably won't be necessary,' soothed his mother. 'I'll have a go at cleaning it shortly. Now, Sam, can you take the plates below, and the glasses. Don't drop them on top of the pavlova.'

'What time can we have the pavlova, Mum?' said Jane.

'You've got a one-track mind,' said Sam, gathering up the plates and shaking the crumbs into the calm sea. Just at this moment she couldn't eat another thing.

'In about half an hour, how's that? It's not quite seven now.'

75

'Can we have a sip of beer then?' Jane's sharp eyes had noticed that Mum didn't seem to want the rest of her beer. They were each allowed a single swig, monitored by the other two.

'You finish it, Dad,' said Jane.

'Gee, thanks,' said Mr Starr draining the almost empty can.

'Pleasure,' said Jane. 'I'm going on the bowsprit again.'

'Life-jacket,' said Mrs Starr automatically.

'Do I have to? I couldn't possible fall off in this weather.'

'Life-jacket, Jane.' Although Mr Starr's voice hadn't altered from its normal pitch, it was very firm. Jane's eyes rolled heavenwards in exasperation, a habit Sam knew irritated her mother; fortunately she was looking aloft and hadn't noticed. Jane squeezed past Sam in the tiny area which passed for a galley just inside the hatchway and got her life-jacket from the bunk.

'Are you going to help Sam with the dishes, Jeremy?' Mrs Starr said as Jeremy also started below.

'Nope. I'm reading,' he said flatly. 'I need to rest my poor bloody head.' He flung himself on the starboard bunk, dislodging a startled Stormy. 'Oh sorry, cat.'

Sam looked at Jeremy with distaste, deciding to ignore him. There were hardly any dishes to do anyway, not until they'd eaten the pavlova. She stood looking out the narrow window above the sink, towards the rocky shoreline of Rangitoto. The silence was intense, broken only by the gurgle of water along the hull. Then she heard a rare sound: her mother laughing, sharing some joke with Dad. How pretty she is when she's not being grim and bossy and sorting out arguments, thought Sam looking up at her. One side of her face was lit gold by the western sun; her bare legs were outstretched and her hand relaxed on the tiller. Behind her, Dad sat with his knees propped up like a grasshopper, playing the spinnaker to catch every little shift of wind.

Sam felt their strength and their dependability as she stood looking up through the hatchway. Smiling, her mother looked down. 'Come up here and enjoy the evening, Sam. You can have a turn steering if you like.'

CHAPTER 9

A wind change

After eight! They had been racing over two hours now. The evening sun still shone warmly on the back of Sam's neck as she sat at the tiller. She gave a huge stretch. This was the life. Free of school, of people, all those strange faces, of traffic, Mum in a good mood, the boat taking them to Kawau. Tomorrow, after a lie-in and a swim off the boat before breakfast, they would go looking for wallabies and wekas on the island.

On the dot of half past seven – Jane had seen to that, although how she *knew* it was half past seven intrigued them all; it was intuition, she said smugly – Mrs Starr dispensed the pavlova with her usual comments about 'sickly stuff, all calories and no taste!' Nonetheless, she served herself a piece and seemed to enjoy it as much as anyone. That over, the family settled down again to a long silence, Jane and Jeremy reading on the bunks below and Sam and her parents in the cockpit.

The wind seemed to be lighter than ever. Sam became aware of a growing sense of isolation. The world had shrunk; it consisted only of *Aratika* and her crew on a little patch of sea. The other boats were illusions, ghost ships, too far away now to distinguish sail numbers. Some had chosen to keep further to the west, closer to the East Coast beaches and out of the tidal stream; most, like the Starrs, had passed within a few hundred metres of the red and white striped Rangitoto lighthouse. They seemed to be holding their own, but Sam knew that the newer, lighter boats would inevitably draw ahead and that from now on it would be difficult to tell how they stood in the race until they sailed past the committee boat in Bon

Accord Harbour. Each yacht would follow its own course through the summer night.

Ahead, but mostly astern, the great fleet spread its sails as far as the eye could see. Occasionally glancing behind to check the surface of the water for ruffles of wind, as Dad had taught her to do, Sam could see a throng of tiny spinnakers, round and bright as lollipops. Those would be the Fourth, Third, Second and finally the sleek giants of the First Division. But there were no little puffs sneaking up from behind; the wind seemed to have dropped to a point where Dad was having difficulty in keeping the spinnaker full. *Aratika* was barely making way through the water. All Sam could do, as helmsman, was hold the tiller steady and keep her on course for Tiri passage. Her eyelids were dropping, like the spinnaker.

'The tide is ebbing,' said her father suddenly. He must have seen her head nodding. 'Eight o'clock tide, so it's just past slack water. That will help a bit. It flows through the passage at a fair clip.'

Jerked out of her half-sleep, Sam peered ahead over the top of the upturned dinghy. The fleet would soon thread itself through the narrow passage between the mainland and Tiritiri Island. Already the powerful Tiri light was sending its flash around the sky every fifteen seconds.

Sam felt a sudden chill as she watched the final sliver of sun disappear behind the western ranges. The sea, although calm enough, had lost its friendliness and was now a sinister molten grey, streaked with lemon and pink. Her small world seemed even smaller. She became very conscious of her father's strength. At home, Mum might be the pivot around which the household revolved, but on the boat Dad was the skipper, who had the last word. She felt she could face anything, the wildest storm, the most magnificent waves, as long as Dad was in charge.

She shivered. 'Can I go and get a jumper, Mum?'

'It's all right. I'll get them, Sam. We're all going to need one soon.' Mrs Starr disappeared into the now murky cabin below. 'Jeremy seems to be fast asleep,' came the low voice.

'That's good,' said Mr Starr. 'Give him a chance to rest that head. Hopefully, he'll sleep right through the night. Tuck him up well, Mum. What's Jane doing? Asleep too?'

'Reading with her pocket torch. Not doing her eyes any good,' said Mrs Starr, reappearing at the hatchway with an armful of jumpers. 'Don't you think we'd better get that spinnaker down, Nick? It'll be dark in about fifteen minutes, maybe less.'

'Won't we get left behind?' asked Sam. 'We'll be the only boat in the fleet without a spinnaker. Can't we take it down later?'

Her father sighed. 'I think your mother's right, Sam. If we'd had Terry we'd have been able to carry it right through to Kawau. Pity. But we won't do too badly under the main and big jenny, you'll see.' He temporarily cleated the spinnaker sheet, stood up on the after deck and yawned noisily.

Sam looked sadly up at the big sail and then at the rest of the fleet. All around them red, white and green lights were appearing like glow-worms against the darkening sea.

'Can you put the navigation lights on before you come up, Mum?' Dad said, both arms raised to the sky in a prolonged stretch. 'I hope . . .'

He stopped abruptly, squinting at the leading boats now passing through the Tiri passage.

'What on earth . . .?'

Sam, alerted, looked up at her father's large shape outlined against the pale lemon sky. He was now pulling on his jumper with a purposeful air.

'What is it, Dad?'

'I should have noticed this earlier. You wouldn't

believe it! Those boats ahead have picked up quite a northerly. Look at them, hard on the wind. God knows where it's come from!'

'A northerly? There was nothing in the forecast about northerlies.' Mrs Starr sounded peevish. She liked things to be orderly and predictable.

The tiny sails of the Sixth Division a couple of kilometres ahead were unmistakably heeled to a northerly. Sam knew what that meant: a long beat all the way to Kawau and hardly the quiet race they had expected.

'We've less than five minutes to get the spinnaker down before we catch that wind, Mum,' said Mr Starr, loosening off the spinnaker guy, then swinging himself monkey-fashion along the deck until he disappeared into the half-light. After the long period of inactivity and calm, Sam felt thrown off balance and suddenly uneasy as helmsman.

'You take her, Mum,' she said plaintively.

'Just a minute, Sam.' She called for'ard. 'Nick? Do you want me to help you with the spinnaker?' She didn't sound too eager about it, thought Sam.

'I could help Dad,' said Sam quickly. Of the two options, she would rather help her father on the foredeck than be in charge of the tiller when the wind changed.

'No thanks,' came a voice from behind the upturned dinghy. 'I can operate better on my own. You take the tiller, Mum. You, Sam, be ready to let go the spinnaker guy when I tell you. And get the lifelines out of the port locker, Sam. We might need them later.'

Sam thankfully handed over the tiller and headed below.

'What's going on?' asked Jane sleepily.

'There's a northerly coming,' said Sam, feeling the lifelines neatly coiled in their usual place in the locker. She put them on the floor just at the foot of the steps where they would be easy to find later on. 'We've got to get the spinnaker down. Or rather Dad has.'

'He's making enough noise about it. What's he *doing* up there?' said Jane as the cabin resounded to three or four heavy thuds and bangs above them. 'Sounds like an elephant.'

'I don't know. That might be the spinnaker pole, I suppose.'

'Sounds like he dropped it.'

'We'd soon know if he did,' said Sam, climbing back into the cockpit.

Her mother was looking anxious, and surprisingly the spinnaker was still up and drawing. Sam had expected to find it down, and Dad busy tidying things up on the foredeck.

'Jane,' Mrs Starr was calling in her best fusspot voice. 'We're going to be tacking. Can you check that Jeremy isn't going to fall out of his bunk. Stuff some cushions under him.'

'I was just going to sleep,' grumbled Jane.

'Weren't we all?' said Mrs Starr tartly. 'Look at that wind on the water, Sam.' Advancing slowly across the leaden sea was a clear line, dark as charcoal, where the wind was ruffling the surface into little short waves. Even as she looked, Sam felt a whisper brush past her cheek and *Aratika* make a slight curtsey to port, the spinnaker restless.

'What's holding up Dad?' said Mrs Starr.

'I don't know.' The spinnaker was still full, but any minute now it would surely collapse, caught aback by the advancing northerly. 'Does he need a torch?'

'It might help. Ask him. There's obviously something he's having to sort out first, although I can't imagine what.' Again the yacht heeled to another puff of wind, this time collapsing the spinnaker and disturbing all the saucepans in the galley below. Sam stood on the cockpit seat and leaned forward over the cabin top. Strangely, there was no movement to be seen anywhere on the foredeck.

'Dad? Do you want a torch?' In the shadows behind the upturned dinghy and the solid wooden mast, it was impossible to see what he was doing. 'Dad! Can I bring you a torch?' she called.

Again there was no response. Sam suddenly realized that there had been no movement on the foredeck since those earlier thuds. Perplexed, she turned and looked at her mother.

'Nick, what's the delay?' shouted Mrs Starr. 'We're going to be caught aback if you don't get that spinnaker down. I'm going to have to run off or something . . .' Just at that moment, a flash from the Tiri light not far away to their right lit up her mother's face. She was standing at the tiller, very tense. Her eyes were wide with fear. Sam knew the same thought had struck them simultaneously.

'Dad,' wailed Sam for'ard into the gloom. Again there was no sound apart from the rustling of the spinnaker as it filled and strained, collapsed and drooped, and filled again. Sam turned back to face her mother.

'He's not there, Mum. He's gone. He's fallen overboard.'

CHAPTER 10

Panic stations

In all their years of sailing, Sam had never seen her mother react so fast. 'Take the tiller, Sam,' she snapped, abandoning the cockpit, oblivious of family rules about life-jackets, lifelines and the rest. The darkness swallowed her up as she too climbed for'ard, leaving Sam grasping the tiller with both hands as much to support her shaking arms as to steer the boat. Above her the great white mainsail, still loosened right out, loomed faintly, catching the last glow from the western sky.

Dad, what's wrong, where are you? If you're not on the foredeck, where are you? Instinctively, she looked behind into the black hissing wake. Even if Dad was swimming around back there somewhere, the moment for seeing him or hearing him, or throwing him the lifebelt, had long since passed. She knew from the man overboard drill they did two or three times every summer just how fast a boat draws away from anyone or anything overboard. But surely they would have heard the splash, or a cry for help. Perhaps he had just slid into the water. Skippers don't fall overboard, especially at night. And, if he had, who was going to sail the boat to Kawau . . . ?

'Mum!' she screamed. The Tiri light lit up the boat again. Still there was no sign of life on the foredeck. Again Sam felt the strain on the tiller as *Aratika* caught another northerly gust, strong enough this time to fold the spinnaker back on itself. 'Mum,' she cried, 'where are you, what's happening?' Now the mainsail as well as the spinnaker was heaving and flapping; the boom was lifting, impatient for a stronger hand on the tiller. 'Mum, come back, I can't hold her any more.' Tears blurred her eyes. The new wind had reached them, an unmistakable steady northerly. She looked desperately around, but the smudged outlines of navigation lights from a hundred boats stared back coldly.

'Sam, why are you yelling? Where's Mum? What's going on?' Jane's face appeared, a pale oval in the hatchway. 'Where's Dad?' She shone her torch into Sam's face.

'Get that thing out of my eyes,' said Sam savagely.

'Where are they?' persisted Jane. 'Tell me.'

'I don't know. They're up front.' She was finding it difficult to shape her words. 'Mum suddenly shot . . . up front. She thinks . . . she thinks Dad has fallen overboard.'

As the Tiri light swept around again – only the second time since Mrs Starr had left Sam at the tiller thirty seconds before – the two sisters looked at each other with dawning horror.

'But we can't sail this great heavy boat without Dad,' said Jane flatly.

'We might have to,' said Sam, tears surging up again. 'Mum!' she shrieked as *Aratika* heeled over alarmingly and veered off to the west on a reach. She hauled at the tiller. 'Help me. I can't hold . . .' A new thought had struck her with the force of a sledgehammer: what if they had both gone over the side?

To her profound relief, another ghostly face appeared abruptly, this time over the top of the upturned dinghy.

'Sam, stop yelling,' Mrs Starr called harshly, 'and just keep her going as she is. For God's sake, don't let her come head to wind, whatever you do. I've got to let the spinnaker fly . . .' The voice trailed off as the face vanished.

'But what about Dad?' said Jane who had leapt up to join Sam in pulling hard on the tiller. Sam felt the warmth of her arms and legs against her own chilled body. In another flash of the Tiri light, they glimpsed below them the end of the main boom tracing a white wake through the water, and the spinnaker straining tautly, far out to port, against its too-tight ropes. Sam, braced rigid, felt she was being pressed slowly over by some unseen force, some giant arm wrist-wrestling with the mast . . . and winning, while *Aratika* surged on through the dark. She was conscious only of the need to pull and pull and pull until either she or *Aratika* gave way. 'It's not fair,' she heard Jane mutter alongside her. 'It's not fair. This boat's too bloody heavy. We can't do this much longer.'

Just as she spoke, there was a sudden pizzicato ping from the foredeck, followed by a silken rushing sound joining the creaks of protesting wood. Sam felt rather than saw the spinnaker fly up into the night to swish around there like a grotesque flag. The pole, freed from the restraint of the lower corner of the sail, began an irritable repetitive thud somewhere. At the same moment *Aratika* shook herself free of the wind. Immensely relieved, Sam was now able to reduce her grip on the tiller and search the darkness ahead. Her main question had still not been answered.

'Mum, tell me what's going on? What's happened to Dad?' she called despairingly.

At last Mrs Starr reappeared in the faint glow cast down by the red and green navigation lights high up on the mast. She was leaning across the dinghy towards the cockpit; her voice was staccato and hard, quite unlike even the brisk tones familiar to Sam.

'Listen both of you. Dad has knocked himself out. It doesn't matter how. We've got to get this boat under control and Dad below. Jane, get the lifelines. The locker above the chart table.' For once, Jane disappeared without comment, her torch picking a tiny hole in the cabin darkness.

86

'Where is he, Mum?' said Sam. 'Won't he come round soon?'

'Not a hope. He's all tangled up in the starboard liferails, out for the count. I've felt his pulse. It's fast, but at least he's not dead and he didn't fall over the side. He might have concussion.'

Stunned, Sam gripped the tiller again and sat down. Her big strong Dad, out cold? And Mum, whose intuition had been right, who hadn't wanted to come on the night race, in charge? It wasn't happening. If only she could turn the clock back.

Above the general clamour of uncontrolled sails, flying ropes and the spinnaker pole banging aggressively against the forestay, her mother was shouting again. 'Sam, can you hear me? I want you up here with me. Jane will have to sail the boat. Has she got those safety harnesses yet?'

'Jane,' called Sam into the dark cabin. 'Mum wants you, quick.'

'I can't find the lifelines.'

'She can't find the lifelines, Mum.'

'Ye gods!' Mrs Starr leapfrogged neatly over the dinghy into the cockpit and disappeared below. 'Use your eyes, child. Here, give me the torch.'

'I have, Mum. I've looked in all the lockers.'

'Put the cabin light on.'

'We can't wake Jeremy, Mum. We don't want him grizzling around.'

True, thought Sam. Mum couldn't argue with that. She could see the torch beam casting around the cabin, then she heard a muffled exclamation from Jane.

'Here they are.'

'Where?'

'On the floor. Dad must have got them out earlier.'

'Sorry, I did,' said Sam. 'I forgot.'

'Oh sure,' said Mrs Starr wearily, climbing back into

the cockpit. 'Now listen, Jane. You've got to take the tiller while Sam and I cope up front.'

There was a brief silence, while Mrs Starr untangled the two safety harnesses and lines in the light of Jane's torch.

'You know I hate steering,' said Jane finally.

'I know we're in big trouble if we don't get that spinnaker off very soon.'

'I'd rather help you with that.'

'I'd rather have Sam. She's stronger,' said Mrs Starr bluntly, pulling on her harness. She fumbled for the mainsheet and hauled the boom in to its correct reaching position. 'That's better. The wind's pretty steady now. Just keep her going as she is. Oh, my God! What's that buoy doing there?'

They all three peered ahead at a small buoy flashing insistent triplets of light at them.

'That's not very far away, Mum,' said Sam. 'What is it?'

'Probably the end of the Whangaparaoa peninsula. Whatever, we haven't much time. We can't do anything until we get that spinnaker off. Sam, hand over, quick. Get that safety harness on.' She started for'ard.

'Here, Jane,' Sam gave her the tiller. Now it would be Jane's turn to feel exposed, small and weak at the helm. 'You'll be okay. We haven't got the jib up, only the main.' Her chilled fingers were having difficulty fastening the clasp on the harness.

'Sam, I hate this. I'm scared.' Jane's voice was subdued.

'I know. So'm I.'

She gathered up the thin line attached to the safety harness, looped it over her arm, and began to climb for'ard along the wet deck, stopping only to clip the end of the line onto the shrouds. It wasn't just the risk of working on the foredeck with all those flapping-flicking ropes waiting to get her in the eye, or the prospect of being dragged along like a fish if she herself slipped and fell overboard. She knew she didn't want to see, even in

88

the shadows, her father's limp body, his pale face with eyes closed, unreachable. She had never seen anyone unconscious before. He would look dead. Perhaps he really was dead, and Mum had said all that about feeling his pulse just to hide the truth. She felt her way around the mast and, despite herself, crouched beside the dark bundle piled up against the starboard liferails. In the faint greenish light, she could just make out his face, which looked as lifeless as she feared. Her fingers smoothed back the wet hair. That was some bump; it felt egg-shaped beneath her cupped hand. But at least she also felt a faint warmth. She was going to cry.

'Sam, have you clipped yourself on? Come *on*.' Her mother was standing by the mast. 'God, how I hate spinnakers. I suppose I let go that other rope first.' As she bounded back to the cockpit to let go the guy, Sam stared up vacantly at the flogging sail, her brain numb, her heart sinking. It was too big for them. Only Dad could handle spinnakers.

'Here, Sam,' her mother was saying impatiently, back on the foredeck. 'I want you to loosen off the spinnaker halyard slowly. I'll bring it in.' She had already cleared the coiled rope so that it would run smoothly up the mast. Sam undid all but the last turn, then to her horror the rope began to slip hotly through her hands, away from her, upwards with increasing speed.

'Hold it, Sam,' yelled Mrs Starr, frantically trying to catch the descending sail. The wind was keeping it just out of arm's reach. 'Keep a turn on the winch.'

'I can't.' She just couldn't grab hold of that burning, slithering rope.

'Oh, hell. That's done it.' Sam looked helplessly at her mother's dark form, swinging like a gymnast as far out as she dared from the port shrouds, vainly attempting to catch one of the ropes or part of the spinnaker itself. The halyard went relentlessly on up the mast as the sail came down, curling itself wickedly around the spreaders, the shrouds, and into the water. Oh Mum, I'm sorry, I'm sorry, I'm sorry. I tried.

'Try pulling it up again, Sam,' came her mother's grim voice.

Sam gave a mighty heave, but the halyard was caught somewhere aloft and would move neither up nor down. Now what? she thought. She looked vainly at the black bundle that was her father – there would be no help from him this night. There were boats on all sides, but they were useless, and that buoy was undeniably closer than the last time she looked. Thoughts of shipwreck flashed through her mind, rocks tearing holes, waves crashing down, Dad sinking silently to the seabed, her own body being dashed and scraped against the oysters . . .

There seemed to be another problem. She was startled back into reality by a tremendous shout from her mother, an unbelievable roar of outrage and fright. Sam had no idea her mother could produce such a noise.

'Staaaaaaarboard,' she bellowed off over the port bow into the night. And sure enough another yacht – a big one – had materialized out of the dark, its green light and shadowy grey sails suddenly at close quarters. *Aratika* surely had right of way, thought Sam in confusion. It was some sort of blatant challenge to hold their course. Sheer bully tactics.

'Starboard, you *fools*.' There was no doubt in her mother's voice. She had to be right.

'Starboard,' echoed Jane's high-pitched wail from the cockpit, betraying the panic of an uncertain helmsman. Sam, still holding uselessly onto the jammed spinnaker halyard, watched as the other boat, not fifteen metres distant, put up a clatter of shouts, of winches singing and sails thundering; then they saw that she had spun off on the other tack. Sam's heart was pounding.

'Hah!' said Mrs Starr, in relief and triumph. 'We've got enough problems without idiots playing chicken.'

'Couldn't they have seen we've still got a spinnaker flapping around?' asked Sam. But even as she spoke she remembered how quickly the other boat had appeared out of the night. Already she had vanished, leaving only a white stern light to remind them of her existence. All those red, green, and white lights surrounding *Aratika* suddenly took on a sinister aspect. With the wind change, the fleet would be crossing tacks all the way to Kawau; even the warning flash from the Tiri light every fifteen seconds couldn't help much, with so many yachts around. People all about, yet Sam couldn't remember ever feeling so lonely.

'Sam, jump to it!'

'What?'

'Go back and help Jane bring the boat onto the wind.'

'Why?'

'For God's sake, Sam, wake up. We're heading straight at that light, whatever it is. We've got to come on the wind and tack soon. Oh, I'll do it,' she said, her voice full of exasperation, starting off back to the cockpit again. 'You try and catch the edge of the spinnaker.'

The spinnaker. As she looked aloft, the white Tiri light obligingly swept over the spinnaker again. She heard the sound of the mainsheet being pulled in through the blocks; *Aratika* was altering course to point north of the buoy. The deck took on a new consistent heel to port as she came hard on the wind.

'Sam, can you grab the spinnaker now?' shouted her mother. Yes, perhaps she could.

'I think so. I'll try.'

'Okay, start grabbing. I'm coming.'

Sam reached downwards to find a shroud or something to brace herself against. Half sitting, half sliding, she swung herself down to the port liferails. If only she could see. She felt for a firm footing, then reached out and down to grab the slithery sail. One handful – but it immediately jumped out of her grasp.

She tried a second time, then a third, but the wind seemed to take a delight in snatching the silken fabric from her cold fingers. Angry and determined, she lunged out, leaning further over the liferails and grabbed at a piece of sail with both hands. Now she was suspended away from the boat, the wire rail biting across her thighs, her arms outstretched. For a long moment she was unable to move, but she was not going to let go of that damn sail, even though her arms felt as if they were being slowly torn from her body. Then she heard a clatter behind her and felt her mother pressing close as she also reached for the nearest shred of sail. Together they started pulling inwards, upwards and down.

'Keep it going, keep it going,' cried Mrs Starr. 'Into the for'ard hatch, quick.' But something had stuck. They were pulling against a lead weight. 'What's the matter *now*?'

'Did you clear the halyard, Mum?' panted Sam, pausing with an armful of wet slimy material clasped to her chest and across her face. For an answer, Mrs Starr let go her portion, leaving Sam hanging on grimly by herself like a dog to a trouser leg.

'The halyard's clear,' Mrs Starr called from the vicinity of the mast. 'Something's caught somewhere. We'll have to pull harder. Try again. Pull!'

There was a loud ripping sound aloft.

'It's caught on the spreaders,' said Mrs Starr grimly. 'Dad's going to love us for this. Again.' Rather you than me having to tell him tomorrow, thought Sam unkindly; but her mother was clearly past caring.

'And again. If that's the only bit of gear we damage during the night, we'll be doing quite well,' her mother added.

They gave three or four mighty heaves, while the tearing sounds from above told them they were winning. Now they could pluck whole armfuls of dripping terylene from the sea and bundle it into the black hole of the for'ard hatch, followed by the two long ropes which had once held the lower corners of the spinnaker taut and proud. Sam smoothed the water from her bare thighs and shook out her jumper, conscious of her heart thumping in her ears.

'You get that halyard unclipped, Sam, and hurry.'

'Mum?' Jane's voice was edgy too. 'That light's getting too close.'

'Coming, Jane,' shouted Mrs Starr. Sam, crouching over the last of the spinnaker, fumbled with the clip which attached it to the halyard. She felt crushed by the sheer weight of the old boat, the blackness of everything, the problems they had still to sort out. The spinnaker pole, hanging from its one wire and pounding hard against the forestay with every movement of the boat, was the first priority. Oh Dad, she cried silently to the still form at her feet, why couldn't you have been more careful?

'Sam, stay there.' Her mother was shouting from the cockpit again. 'Ready about. Lee-o!' She felt *Aratika* straighten up as Mrs Starr steered her through the eye of the wind, then bend gracefully to her new north-eastern course. Shifting her own balance, Sam instinctively stretched out her arm to stop her father's lifeless form sliding off downhill into the water. She had a sudden clear image of his limp body being swept away while she vainly tried to cling to his cold fingers. She wouldn't be strong enough to hold him. In terror she grabbed a handful of wet jumper, then realized that her father had merely settled further against the liferails. What was it that William had said about liferails, before breakfast, centuries ago?

She bent again to the clip, finally freeing the slack

halyard. What next? Her brain felt as cold as her fingers. Do something with the halyard, she told herself, like clip it back into the mast somewhere; secure the hatch over the last of that beastly spinnaker. There was a tangle of ropes beneath her bare feet. Her own lifeline seemed to be getting all wound up too. She started to feel along the line leading from her harness; she couldn't remember which part of the rigging she'd clipped it to. She was a fly in a spider's web of ropes and rigging.

'You okay, Sam?' Her mother's urgent voice in her ear made her jump. 'We can't get that spinnaker pole in until we've moved Dad below. It gets stowed right where he's lying.'

Sam had been dreading this more than any of the many unpleasant tasks that undoubtedly lay ahead. She didn't want to have to help pull her father's unconscious form around the boat, his head lolling about and his arms and legs all floppy. He could be a dead body for all she knew.

'I'm just untangling my lifeline, Mum. It's all caught up.'

'Well, do it then.'

'I *am*.'

'You'll have to hurry.'

'Why? We're not heading for any rocks and . . .' She was going to say there were no boats anywhere near them, but as she looked over towards the Tiri light and back towards Auckland she realized she would be talking nonsense. The sea was full of lights and every one was a threat.

'Which way are we going to take him?'

'Into the cockpit, of course.'

'Why not down the for'ard hatch? It's not nearly so far.'

'Because,' said her mother tetchily, 'that's all full of spinnaker, as you well know. Anyway, even without the spinnaker it'd be too difficult to get him past the mast into

94

the cabin. You know how squashed it is at the best of times.'

The lifeline cleared, Sam reluctantly slid on her haunches down towards her father. Mrs Starr had already got her hands under his shoulders and had lifted him to a half-sitting position like a rag doll.

'Sam for heaven's sake, help me. I can't do this by myself.'

'There isn't room for both of us. The boom's in the way if we go back that side. *And* the dinghy,' she added sullenly, searching the blackness for a way out. Then, in the Tiri flash, she saw her mother's eyes were pleading with her. She needs me, thought Sam in surprise, she actually needs me, not just for babysitting Jeremy or peeling potatoes or the other boring jobs I do to help, but because I'm *strong*, and we've got to get out of this mess together.

'Okay then,' her mother was saying, her voice tightly controlled, 'you may be right. We'll have to drag him around the mast and up along the windward side.' She yelled suddenly in the direction of the cockpit, making Sam jump. 'Jane? You're lookout. We're on port tack, it's up to us to give way. You keep your eyes peeled for any lights coming near. *Anywhere* near, do you understand?'

'Do I look for red lights or green?' shouted Jane.

'Oh hell, I don't know, Jane.' She sounded flustered. 'Work it out . . . oh, it'll be red lights, I suppose. Yes, red lights, to starboard.'

Poor Jane, thought Sam – terrified of steering, as she herself would be if she were really honest – and now lookout as well. But what else could Mum do until they got Dad safely below – apart from dragging Jeremy up on deck to be extra lookout, and he would be more trouble than he was worth. Against the soft loom of the city's lights in the southern sky, she could see her mother's profile clearly. Sam guessed she was taking a calculating look at the time before one of those red lights forced them to go about.

'We'll be all right for a few minutes at least, Sam,' Mrs Starr said finally, her tone more composed. 'Now, you take one shoulder and I'll take the other.'

Sam felt the solid mass of her father's chest as she slipped her hand beneath his armpit and tried to get a grasp on the wet wool of the jumper. It was no use. She had to kneel down and bend over further to get a firmer hold, to bend so close that she could smell the faintly doggy smell of his wet hair and hear clearly his unnaturally shallow breathing.

'Ready? Heave!' her mother called. Sam took the strain, pulling upwards and back; they moved him about ten centimetres.

'Again,' gasped her mother.

Slowly, gaining only a little with each effort, they lugged the limp body up the angled deck, across the hatch cover, and across the tangle of ropes around the foot of the mast. Sam didn't know how much her father weighed, but it was twice as much as she expected. Various ropes hooked themselves viciously around their bare feet as they both searched the wet deck for firm footholds against which to brace their trembling legs for the next heave. Then Sam found herself hard up against the dinghy and cried out for a rest. She pulled herself upright, grasping at the port shrouds, gasping for breath.

'Mum,' she panted. 'You've got to manage the next bit. There isn't room for both of us.' The passage along the deck between the dinghy and the liferails was barely wide enough for a child to walk. In the very faint reddish glow from the port light above, she could see her mother's shoulders heaving. She was half-crouched, half-propped against the dinghy with Dad draped untidily across her knees. Her face seemed to be buried in Dad's curly matted hair.

'Mum? Are you all right? Mum!' Sam thought she heard a strange sound coming from the two intertwined forms. Was it Dad coming round . . . or Mum crying?

Her answer was a long resolute sniff. 'Yes. I'm all right, Sam.' Again the voice was cool, betraying no sign of any crack in the outward show of confidence. She was wiping her nose along the back of her jumper. 'I'm glad your father's not built like a front-row forward. I don't think we could manage if he was.'

'How are you going to get him along there?'

'Slowly. The best I can.' In the brief pause, Sam could see her mother's head again lowered, almost embracing Dad as though she was trying to draw on some of his strength. Then she struggled to find a foot purchase for the next effort. 'You might be able to lift his legs.'

Somehow they inched their way aft, Mrs Starr taking all Dad's weight against her chest as she backed along the narrow space, with Sam lifting as much as she could of his wet bare legs, their texture rough with goosepimples. Again she had to push thoughts of corpses from her mind. It was more difficult than before since his legs were deathly cold.

Then progress was held up as they realized that their own lifelines had become confused. The only solution was to take them off completely. Sam felt naked without the lifeline anchoring her firmly to the boat and was glad when she could clip herself to the liferail again. She watched helplessly as her mother resumed the task of easing Dad along the deck. As they approached the cockpit, Sam could just see Jane's little black head; she looked absurdly small. Ten-year-old girls, thought Sam, don't *usually* get put in charge of nine-metre keelers at night, especially old-fashioned ones with bowsprits and running backstays and wooden blocks. Neither, come to think of it, do women.

CHAPTER 11

More panic stations

With her back to the cockpit and her attention given wholly to the task of dragging a tall male body along a confined deck, it was no wonder that Mrs Starr didn't see the second boat to give them trouble until it was very nearly too late. After all, Jane was supposed to be lookout. Perhaps their mother had forgotten that Jane was a bit short-sighted; even if she had remembered, thought Sam later, what else could she have done?

Sam, engrossed in trying to help where she could, thought she heard a shout. A male shout. Puzzled, she glanced up. Her mother, obviously tiring, was grunting loudly with each separate heave. There it was again. She peered around the dinghy, to check. She and Jane must have seen the boat at the same time, for they both yelled 'Mum!' at the top of their lungs. And Sam heard another shout, closer this time: an unmistakable male voice bawling 'Starboard' just as her mother had done half an hour earlier. The boat, clearly visible now, was even closer than the yacht they themselves had yelled at.

Mrs Starr didn't bother to shout at anyone. She dropped Dad's head and shoulders on the deck and dived for the tiller, pushing it hard over with the weight of her body. Jane, thrust roughly aside, gave a cry of pain. *Aratika* wheeled around onto a course parallel with the other yacht, her boom crashing over while Mrs Starr strained desperately at the backstays. From for'ard came the sickening thud of the still unsecured spinnaker pole against the forestay. Sam, without thinking, threw herself down on the soft cushion of her father's body, mainly, she realized later, an unconscious reaction to avoid being knocked off the boat by the heavy boom. Together they rolled further down against the liferails as *Aratika* settled onto the new tack.

Sam was shaking uncontrollably, her heart thud, thud, thud, thudding against her eardrums, her eyes filling with tears. She buried her face in her father's wet jumper, conscious of the rapid movements of his chest and his harsh breathing. She cautiously lifted her head, feeling as though a bomb had gone off. Why wasn't Mum asking that other boat for help? It was so close, she could tell them all their troubles. Then, above the usual noises of a yacht under way, she heard the voice: male and angry, pouring a stream of abuse on *Aratika* as the two yachts ran a parallel course about twenty metres apart.

Incredulous, she propped herself up to see what sort of person could talk like that, but all she could make out was a vague grey smudge against the black sea. The furious skipper was a faint ghost with waving arms. All the words Sam had heard before in the school playground, but the hostility behind them stunned her. Is this how men talk to each other, she wondered. Of course, he wasn't to know that *Aratika* was a family boat, still less that the one man on board was lying unconscious on the deck. She scrambled into the cockpit to join her mother sitting up to windward, their backs to the other yacht, hunched as though sitting in the rain. Mrs Starr appeared to be quietly steering, but moving closer to put a protective arm around her mother's shoulders, Sam could feel that she was trembling violently. With rage? Or disgust? Or was it simply reaction to the near-collision? She couldn't tell.

In the end, it was Jane who silenced him. 'Mum?' she muttered from the lee cockpit seat where she had been thrown. 'Say something, Mum. Mum!' But Mrs Starr either could not or would not respond. 'If you won't, I will.' Just as she stood up, the Tiri light swept around again, briefly disclosing to Sam and her mother a small indignant figure with the gleam of battle in her eyes. From inside her jumper, where it hung on a cord around her neck, she drew her torch and shone it directly into the cockpit of the other boat. It was a special torch, small yet powerful, recently bought with birthday money. Turning round, Sam saw the beam land directly on the helmsman's face. Momentarily blinded, he broke off in mid-sentence, and quickly put an arm up to shield his eyes. It wasn't done, old boy, thought Sam, to use a torch as an aggressive weapon. But before he could protest, Jane had flung two brisk words across the dark sea. She snapped off the torch.

'*Jane*!' Mrs Starr sounded outraged, but Sam could tell it was half-hearted, a mother's automatic reaction. Certainly their opponent had been effectively silenced by the sound of a young, angry female voice speaking the same language. Probably he could hardly believe his ears, smiled Sam to herself.

'Jane, we were in the wrong,' her mother said, without conviction. 'I can't blame him for being angry.'

'Come off it, Mum. Who does he think he is! No one should speak to anyone like that. And we didn't even touch his miserable boat.'

'No thanks to you,' said Sam, half-admiring her younger sister, half-resentful that she had shown more spunk than either Sam or her mother. 'You're a rotten lookout.'

'Oh yes, I get all the blame. I *was* looking. I just didn't think it was so near. I'm short-sighted, remember?'

Sam was silent. Anyone else who'd nearly caused a collision might, she thought, just *might* have said sorry, but not Jane. She was still shaking from the narrowness of their escape, and her mother's shoulders were, if anything, heaving more than ever. Oh no, she wasn't going to cry. Sam couldn't bear the thought of her mother crying; she never cried. But when it came the sound was not of tears, but laughter. Mrs Starr was looking across at the other boat, which was already pulling ahead – and she was laughing.

'Oh, Jane,' Mrs Starr exploded. 'I never . . . oh, you're braver than me. I was brought up to believe . . . that nice girls . . . didn't even *know* words like that.' Sam wished she could see her mother's face clearly. It was usually only with grown-up friends that she laughed like this. A big chuckle welled up inside her, too. Then they were all rocking with laughter, sharing the release of tension as Mrs Starr cried, 'He thought we were men . . . oh dear . . . oh dear me . . .'

'Plain boring, if you ask me,' gasped Jane. 'All that about not putting to sea if you don't know the rules. And not having idiots sticking their bowsprits into *his* fifty-thousand-dollar boat.' She sneezed noisily. 'You know the rules, don't you, Mum?'

The laughing petered away. There was only a brief silence before Mrs Starr spoke. 'I suppose I do,' she said, sniffing. 'Sam, we can't sit here all night. We've got to get Dad below.'

Guiltily, Sam realized that she had, for a minute or two, forgotten all about him lying somewhere along the lee deck. How could she!

'This time I want you to take the tiller, Sam, and Jane to help me. I think it would be best to tack again before we try to shift him. I don't think I could manage to pull him up the hill. So we'll be on port again, Sam, and you're lookout.'

Sam nodded unhappily.

'Do you agree?'

'Course I do.'

'Well, say so. I can't see what you're thinking, can I? It's as black as the ace of spades back here, apart from that damn lighthouse. It's getting on my nerves.'

As she spoke the light swept around the cockpit again,

101

as if to say spitefully, I'm still here, you're going to remember me and this night for ever – and I've seen one or two things in my time, I can tell you. A bell rang in Sam's memory: a big yacht called *Northerner* hit a rock in the Tiri passage and went down in the middle of the night, years ago. She remembered Dad telling her about it quite recently. Where was that rock now, she wondered uneasily?

'Ready about. I'll do the backstays,' Mrs Starr was saying. Instinctively, Sam glanced behind her. Mum, of course, would already have checked that they would not be tacking into the path of one of those nasty red lights. Or had she? Sam stiffened. There was one, not so far away. She *must* have seen it.

'Hold it, Mum.'

'Lee-o,' said Mrs Starr, pushing the tiller away from her.

'No, don't!'

'Why not?' *Aratika* was already pointing into the wind, the mainsail loose and rustling loudly above them.

'Look behind.'

'Dear God,' said Mrs Starr. 'Why didn't you tell me? Now we're in irons.' She pulled the tiller back amidships, but there was no response from *Aratika*. She had lost way and was wallowing. The sea wasn't as calm as it had been.

'Push the tiller the other way, Mum,' said Sam urgently.

'What?'

'The other way. Dad says you push it the other way when you get into irons. The opposite way to what you think.'

'That doesn't make sense,' put in Jane.

'Will you shut up, Jane? Mum, true, the other way.'

Sam had no way of telling whether her mother was grateful or angry, but she pulled the tiller towards her and slowly, so slowly, the bow came round and again *Aratika* heeled over on starboard tack, away from the Tiri light. Sam looked behind to where the red light now clearly belonged to a big First Division keeler, surging powerfully through the short chop. That tight feeling of fear was beginning to knot up her stomach again. At this rate they were bound to do something really stupid before the night was out.

'Thanks, Sam.' Her mother sounded subdued. 'Silly of me.'

'Won't we have to wait until that big boat behind goes about?' Perhaps she had better check ahead. Not so very far away another light flashed its white message at her. As she stood to get a good look over the dinghy, Sam became aware of the sound of surf echoing from the land ahead. She knew it was the end of the peninsula. What she didn't know was how far away that buoy was. But breaking waves could only mean one thing: they would *have* to tack soon.

'What do we do if that boat stays there?' said Jane aggressively. 'Mum, I don't like you being skipper. I want Dad to wake up.'

'Do you think Mum is enjoying this much?' said Sam quickly. 'Or me for that matter?'

'Mum, couldn't we throw some water over Dad's face? Wouldn't that wake him up? It does when people faint on telly.'

Sam was shocked. 'Jane, Dad's got concussion. Don't try to be funny. This is not some big game, you know.'

'Of course I know that.'

'And who was it who said we couldn't sail this heavy great boat without Dad,' accused Sam. 'Well, we have, so far, and no thanks to you nearly causing a collision.'

'Gosh, Sam, that's not fair. I've been steering for hours, and you know how I hate steering.'

'I hate steering,' mocked Sam. 'How do you think Mum feels, having to lump Dad around the boat. And we haven't even got him below yet. How do you think he feels, being knocked out?'

'He's not feeling anything.'

'God, Jane, you're a little beast and . . .'

'Right, that's enough,' came the voice from the helm, low but as urgent as a referee's whistle.

'Honestly, Mum,' appealed Sam. 'She . . .'

'I said enough. While you two have been arguing about nothing, that boat has gone about. See?' Sam looked, her eyes misty with rage. The red light and faint outline of the big keeler was now merely a white stern light heading off on the opposite tack, growing steadily smaller even as she watched.

'Okay, let's tack. Listen to those breakers! Ready on the backstay, Sam? Lee-o.' And they executed their first smooth, controlled, unhurried tack since nightfall. 'Good. Now, Sam, you take the tiller. You are lookout, right?'

Sam moved over to the left side of the cockpit and bracing her bare feet against the opposite seat, grasped the tiller. The boat felt comfortable enough. She sensed that the sea, if only she could see it, was building up into a nasty short chop. Of course, wind against the tide. It wouldn't be long before spray started flying across the decks. She was rather glad that she couldn't see the waves growing bigger before her eyes. It was enough to feel the old yacht beginning to buck and bob. What she could see were all those navigation lights, far too many of them. Watch for the red ones, Mum had said. Whenever they had sailed through the passage by day, it had seemed so wide and clear; this present feeling of being crowded out was very strange to her.

'You'll have to sit right up in the corner, Sam,' her mother was saying, breaking into her thoughts. 'Just until I get Dad below.'

Sam moved aft as much as she could, but even there she

felt jostled as her mother and Jane struggled to lift first his head and shoulders, then the rest of him, over the big brass winch and the cockpit coaming. Sam could hear her mother's breath coming in short gasps even after three or four heaves; again, in the restricted space and with everything on an angle, she was having to do most of the lifting. Sam's heart ached for her mother. It was a horrible job, heaving your husband around in the dark, not knowing how badly hurt he was.

The Tiri light shone dimly on Mrs Starr resting against the hatch, her arms over her head. Somewhere down on the cockpit floor, amongst all the ropes, was Dad. Sam took her foot off the seat and tentatively felt down towards the grating. Her chilled toes came up against some other cold wet flesh: his legs, she guessed. A dead body wouldn't feel any colder. She returned to her steering and her job as lookout.

At long last the lighthouse was beginning to drop astern. Perhaps they were clear of the island. If she followed those white lights ahead she'd be all right, surely. No red lights to speak of, except for a bunch near the lighthouse. If only it wasn't so black everywhere . . .

'Mum,' she said suddenly. 'Can't we put the cabin light on?'

A muffled voice answered. 'It's better for whoever's steering to keep it off. And you know Dad doesn't like to run off the batteries unless we've had a good engine run.'

'For heaven's sake, Mum, isn't this a bit different?' said Sam irritably. 'I want to be able to see what's going on. It's like being blind. I'm sick of all this dark. And you'll want to see what you're doing.'

'Okay.' But still she didn't move.

'Can't you do it, Jane? Use your torch.'

'Do what?'

'Put the cabin light on. Didn't you hear what Mum said?'

'Okay, okay. But I don't need a torch for that.' She groped her way down into the cabin and a few seconds later the light flicked on. Sam blinked. Her eyes had grown so used to the dark that even the feeble cabin light behind its thick ridged glass made her flinch. She could see them both now: a huddled shape, two long bare legs attached to a lifeless body slumped on the cockpit floor, and her slight, tired mother leaning against the hatchway. Past them was the security of the cabin, which suddenly seemed a very desirable place to be, warm and protected from the wind and all those hostile lights and that interminable Tiri light. She could just make out the blanketed shape of Jeremy sleeping peacefully on the starboard bunk. If only she could climb into the other bunk, pull a blanket up over her head and switch herself off. She wanted to slip back three hours in time, to have a second chance. Dad would say no to Jane's bullying about the spinnaker, he wouldn't go on deck to get it down, Mum and Dad would sail the boat to Kawau while she slept . . . and slept . . .

An unseen wave came up over the side and slapped her rudely in the face. She gasped. The sea was rougher, there was no doubt about it. Even under mainsail only, there was a little more weight on the tiller; the bowsprit was dipping deeper. She looked apprehensively around the sky. A few clouds, grey on black, over to the west; cold staring stars; no moon. The wind fingered her hair and stung her wet cheekbones.

'The wind's getting up, Mum.' Her small, frightened voice had an immediate effect on her mother, who swung around and bent again for the final lap.

'Just keep her going as she is, Sam,' she said, preoccupied. 'Jane, come back up, will you? See if you can swing his legs over the step.'

'Let me get past then,' said Jane, climbing back up the ladder. Sam regretted her suggestion about the cabin light. Dad looked so totally lifeless, so grey in the dim shadows. Gradually, they hauled him to the top of the steps. Sam watched, wishing she could help.

'Wait a minute, Mum,' she called. 'Wouldn't it be best to move Jeremy first, into the other bunk? Then you won't have to lift Dad uphill.'

Mrs Starr straightened up, staggering almost as though she were drunk, as a nasty sequence of waves sent a shower of spray across the cockpit. She nodded slowly.

'We don't want to wake Jeremy,' warned Jane.

'It can't be helped. Sam's right. I don't think I could lift Dad uphill into a bunk. I'm damn sure I couldn't.' She swung herself wearily down into the cabin towards Jeremy, who had slept so peacefully through everything. You've got it made, thought Sam, being the youngest and the longed-for male of the species. Sam could see the effort required for her mother to lift the small figure, blankets and all, and then to edge her way around the fixed table between the two bunks and back up to the windward bunk. Jeremy so far had hardly stirred, but when his mother finally deposited him heavily on the uphill bunk, he grunted. His eyes flew open and he half sat up.

'What's going on?' he said loudly. 'What's happening?'

Sam couldn't hear her mother's reply, but she knew it would be all sweet nothings as she leant over Jeremy and fussed around with cushions to make the mattress more level, tucked him up, stroked his forehead, and no doubt whispered things like 'Go back to sleep, everything's fine.' Sam smiled. He would be absolutely furious in the morning, when they were bobbing around peacefully in Bon Accord. Jane, who had also been watching closely from the hatch, silently raised her arms, hands clasped in an Olympic victory salute, as Jeremy slipped back into sleep.

'Bring the cat over, Jane,' said Mrs Starr, but Stormy,

woken from his warm sleep in the crook of Jeremy's knees, was already walking over the table and up onto Jeremy's pillow, there to settle himself down again.

'We mightn't be so lucky next time,' said Mrs Starr. 'We'll have to keep the noise down.' She looked up towards Sam. 'Now. Dad.'

The final stages turned out to be the worst. Jane helped where she could, but there simply wasn't room for them to share the load. Mrs Starr would have made it on her first headlong lunge at the bunk, with Mr Starr draped in a sort of untidy fireman's lift over her shoulders, had it not been for a sudden lurch of the boat, maliciously in the wrong direction. There was confusion for a minute or two, but finally it was done. They rubbed his cold legs with towels and covered him with every blanket they could find. Jane must have been told to lie alongside to warm him with her body heat, for Sam saw her stretch herself ratherly gingerly along what little space that remained of the bunk, and pull the blankets over them both. Sam had the strangest feeling that she was watching an old silent movie, in slow motion. Her mother's movements were more deliberate than ever; and in the pale light there were no colours, only shadows. Even her bright turquoise jumper was drained of colour as she bent awkwardly towards the bunk, over the table, feeling the pulse in Mr Starr's neck.

Sam looked at her watch. Nearly half past ten. It had taken them one and a half hours just to get the spinnaker down, and her father below! And what should – or could – they do next?

CHAPTER 12

'Three useless kids'

Actually Sam was beginning to feel just a little bit cocky. They *had* managed so far, hadn't they – with the spinnaker, with Dad, avoiding collisions left, right and centre, and the only immediate problem still to be dealt with was the spinnaker pole. She was almost enjoying the feel of the old yacht under her hands. It was the same sensation she had enjoyed this summer when sailing the small dinghy: of being in a boat comfortably balanced against a steady breeze and herself in control. She had never been at the helm of *Aratika* on the wind for so long or in such fresh conditions, nor indeed ever at night. It wasn't that Dad hadn't often asked her to steer, but she had always managed to avoid it – and anyway, that was one of the things her mother normally liked doing.

The Tiri light was beginning to lose its jagged brilliance. Sam looked over her shoulder to the north. Now that they were through the passage, there must be plenty of open sea ahead. There seemed to be as many boats ahead of them as behind. She checked again the danger area back towards the lighthouse. A small cluster of red lights appeared closer and more threatening than all the others. They would probably have to tack again in a few minutes.

As she turned to call down into the cabin, she was startled to see her mother rushing towards the hatch, a book in her hand. What now, thought Sam, her rising spirits sinking without trace. Mrs Starr flung herself up the companion-way and down towards the lee rail. The noise was unmistakable. She was being violently and thoroughly sick.

Sam had forgotten her mother's tendency to seasickness. Of course, it was always Dad who went below to get cups of tea when they set out on their weekend trips. Mum took a day at least to get her sea legs. No wonder all that lifting and straining below had proved too much. It was a surprise she had lasted that long. Sam watched helplessly.

'Mum? Are you all right?' But the spasms continued for what seemed like minutes. That tight feeling, so familiar now, was back like a solid lump in Sam's stomach. Mum couldn't get crook as well. She couldn't.

Slowly, Mrs Starr pulled herself back out of the darkness. In the faint glow of the cabin light, Sam could see the saliva dribbling down her chin, the tears in her eyes, her whole body trembling. She looked awful.

'Are you all right?' Sam repeated. It was a silly question, but what else could she say. 'Answer me. You okay?' Sam longed to comfort her, to put her arms around her, but she knew that in this wind she couldn't take her hands off the tiller, even for a moment.

'I'm . . . okay. I will be . . . in a minute. Truly, Sam. I'm usually okay once . . . once I've been sick.' But another spasm shook her, and over the lee rail she went again.

'You don't look too good. Can I get you anything?' asked Sam after a tactful interval.

'All those fish and chips for tea. And pavlova! I knew I shouldn't have eaten any,' she said, wiping her wet forehead with her sleeve. 'It was the reading that finished me.'

'What on earth were you trying to read?' She would have to tell Mum about those boats on starboard, very soon.

'The First Aid book. I really don't know what we should do about Dad next. I hadn't even got as far as the index.' She leant over and picked up the book. 'It's all wet,' she sniffed, moving over to perch at the top of the companion-way so that she could hold the book up to the cabin light behind. There was something odd about her manner, thought Sam, as she opened the book slowly, almost as though she didn't want to know what was inside. 'Here we are. Unconsciousness, page 140, asphyxia, causes of, convulsions, diabetes – that's not it – yes, here, head injury, page 144, fracture of the skull, injury to the brain . . . oh, God. . . .' The book fell to the cockpit floor.

'Don't cry, Mum.'

'I'm sorry, Sam. It's just . . . it's just all too . . .'

Sam turned her eyes away from the sight she couldn't bear to watch, acutely aware of those little red lights getting steadily closer.

'Mum, don't cry. We've got to tack soon.' She was thoroughly rattled. Mum shouted, bossed, ordered people around, sometimes she smiled, joked, cuddled, listened, laughed; but cried? Never. She wasn't one of those simpering ducky ladies with nail polish who never got their hair wet at the beach. She was at this moment the skipper. And skippers didn't cry, especially on and on when there was tacking to be done and rules of the road to be obeyed.

'Mum, there's a whole bunch of red lights coming up. We've got to tack soon . . . now, really . . . please, Mum . . .'

Mrs Starr lifted her wet face. She looked at Sam blankly as though surprised to see her there.

'What did you say?'

'Look there, those red lights.' They both looked back. 'Shouldn't we go about now?'

'Hell, Sam, why didn't you say so earlier?'

'I did.'

'You did not.'

'I did, Mum. You were crying; you wouldn't listen.

111

Here, you take the tiller. I don't want to steer any more.'

'Certainly I'll take the tiller. And I'll do the backstays.' She thrust herself roughly alongside Sam, looking angrily over at the approaching lights, now too close to argue about. Close enough, in fact, to see the faint outline of the boats behind them. 'You should have given me more warning.'

'I tried, Mum . . .'

'Next time give me more warning. Ready about.'

'How could I when . . .'

'Lee-o.' She gave the tiller a vicious thrust. *Aratika* spun around. 'Do you think I want a collision to add . . .'

'Of course not,' shouted Sam through the racket. 'You're not being fair.'

'Fair? Who said anything about being fair? Do you think it was fair . . .' She paused while straining at the windward backstay. '. . . was it fair of your father to bully me into this race? I didn't want to come. I knew something wasn't right. I knew it! But he wouldn't listen, would he? Working on all you kids at breakfast – something special about the night race. You encouraged him, I know. Sneaking along to William's to get the key. We shouldn't have come without Terry. We shouldn't have come at all. It was irresponsible to come at all.'

'How could Dad know . . .'

'That's just it.' She was in full cry now. 'He always knows better. And who is having to pick up the pieces? Who's got to get this boat to Kawau in one piece? Don't you realize that there are reefs and rocks and stuff up there?' As she pointed to the north, a big wave broke against the hull, sending a blast of warm water over to drench them both. Mrs Starr shook the water from her face. 'It's all very well for him, lying down there. He'll just wake up in the morning and start saying how grateful he is and how marvellous we all are. That's if there *is* a morning.'

'What else would you expect him to do?' yelled Sam.

'Watch where he puts his feet next time.'

'Anyone can have an accident.'

'It wasn't an accident. It was irresponsible. Just plain clumsiness, that's all.'

Sam was outraged. 'That's an awful thing to say. That's not fair. Anyone can slip over.'

'We should never have put that spinnaker up.'

'You didn't say anything at the time. Dad asked you. I remember him asking,' she shouted accusingly.

'Oh yes. And if I had said no? You would have bullied me into it, the whole lot of you. I shouldn't have stood a chance.'

Sam was silent.

'And here I am in charge of this great boat, no radio to call for help. I can't work the engine, the wind's getting up and hundreds of boats are in the way.' They both recoiled from another big wave breaking into the cockpit. 'I'm not Naomi James,' she yelled. 'This is a man's boat. It needs a crew of three men in these conditions, minimum – not three useless kids.'

'We've done all right up till now,' Sam hurled back. 'You aren't fair on anybody. I'm not useless. I can steer as well as you. I'll do anything you want. Like that spinnaker pole,' she said defiantly, conscious of the dull thud the pole was still making against the forestay.

'You couldn't, Sam. You're not strong enough. It's too heavy.' Suddenly she sounded deflated, her anger spent.

'I don't care. Throw it over the side.'

'And sink another boat which runs over it?'

Sam's mind was a turmoil of outrage, fright and complete helplessness. She couldn't help being only twelve and female and weak.

'I've had enough of this,' she wailed. 'I'm frozen and I'm wet and I wish we'd never come on this horrible race. I hate sailing at night and I'm scared, and I want Dad to wake up and tell us what to do because you don't know and you're not a proper skipper . . .'

Her voice trailed off as she caught the expression in her mother's eyes. So sad and hurt. Sam burst into tears and rolled herself into a tight little ball in the lee corner of the cockpit, out of the glow of the cabin light. She didn't want to see or hear anything.

There was a long silence, broken only by a muffled inquiry from Jane below as to what was going on. 'Nothing to worry you, Jane,' said Mrs Starr flatly. Sam, her head buried in her arms, sniffing loudly, heard only her mother's wounded retreat into silence and the eerie slap of the waves against the hull.

'I'm sorry, Mum,' she mumbled eventually. 'I didn't mean it like that. I'm so cold and . . . oh . . . I get scared when you cry and talk about rocks. We've had so many frights, I'm feeling all confused.'

'So am I,' said Mrs Starr quietly. 'I'm hating every minute of this. But you and me . . . we're in charge. We've got a boat and five people to cope with. I know I'm not much of a skipper . . .'

'I really didn't . . .'

'No, you're right. I've never actually been in charge of a boat in my life. Apart from sailing the dinghy, that is. I should have. Dad and I should have talked about what we'd do, or what I'd do, in this situation. We've concentrated only on what we'd do if one of you kids fell over. Never this. I've always meant to do a boatmaster's course or something. Your father's been sailing since he was a child. He can rely on instinct and experience to get him through. I can't.'

She was almost talking to herself.

'I suppose in five summers of sailing, something should have rubbed off. Naomi James hadn't done even that when she sailed off around the world, and she made it.' She looked straight at Sam. 'We will too. But I can't – I

114

won't – on my own. I need your help, Sam.' Her voice was calm and matter-of-fact. Listening to her, Sam in a strange way felt stronger; it was good to be needed.

'Now you take the tiller. I've got to fix that spinnaker pole, then we can talk about what we're going to do.' Mrs Starr bent down and started to untangle the safety harness and lifelines caught up in the heap of ropes on the cockpit floor. 'Dad wouldn't think much of this, for a start.'

'Can I change my jumper and get an oilie first?' said Sam. It was going to be a wet night. The waves were breaking with increasing frequency against the hull and sending spray across the cockpit.

'Good idea. I'll change mine after I've done the spinnaker. Have a look at Dad while you're down there. And pass me the torch, just inside the door. I'll try again with the book.'

Sam climbed carefully down into the cabin. There was a strong smell of wet wool and damp bodies.

'That you, Sam?' came Jane's small voice from the uphill bunk. 'I don't like it on this tack. Dad's pushing me right up against the table. What was all that shouting?'

'Nothing. Just Mum getting shirty. She's all right now.' It was good to get her wet clothes off and pull on a clean T-shirt and dry jumper. 'Mum wants to know how Dad is. Any change?'

'No.'

'Is he warming up?'

'Yes, but I'm squashed.'

Sam, her oilskin on, peered over the table at the two figures on the bunk. 'You are, too. Hop up and we'll stuff some cushions underneath.' She pulled out a couple of spare cushions from under the pile of spinnaker in the fore cabin. They were damp, but wasn't everything? 'We'll have to roll him back a bit first.' Pushing Mr Starr uphill took all their combined muscle power, but they managed to get the cushions under the mattress.

'That's better,' said Jane. 'Now I can breathe.'

'You're sure there's no sign of Dad waking up?'

'I'm sure.'

Sam looked down at them both, reluctant to leave the security of the cabin for the wet and scary night outside; but she too was beginning to feel sick, so to linger was probably unwise. What could she take up to Mum to make her feel better? Food, drink? Her eye caught the First Aid box which Mum had left open on the bench in the galley. She poked through the jumble of plasters, scissors, sterile dressings, little bottles of pills and tubes of cream, before her fingers felt a larger bottle. She held it up to the light, where it glowed deep gold. Brandy, the label said, for medicinal purposes only! What better?

'Here, Mum,' she smiled, climbing back into the cockpit, brandy bottle in hand. 'Brought you a present.'

'What's this?'

'Brandy. From the First Aid kit.'

'Well done. I'd quite forgotten it was there.'

'Have some.'

'Not yet, I'm afraid,' she said. 'I've got to get that wretched pole down first.' She had already put her safety harness on over her soggy jumper. 'Now, Sam, we don't have to worry about rocks or lighthouses for a while, and we're on starboard, so just keep her going as she is. But don't relax your lookout. Don't trust anyone.'

'What colour would the lights be on this tack, Mum?' She inspected the black horizon where fewer red and green lights could now be seen through the driving spray. There seemed to be more white stern lights up to the north, which could mean only one thing – that most of the race yachts, surging along under big jibs and sailing closer to the wind than *Aratika*, had already overtaken them.

'What colour?' Mrs Starr paused to work it out, using her hands as models. 'We're going along on starboard, like this. Boat on port, like this. It would be his . . . green

116

light we see? That makes sense, doesn't it, Sam? His green light? Yes. I'm not thinking too well.'

'Sounds okay.' Sam moved to take over the tiller, making herself comfortable on the wet seat, snug inside her dry jumper and oilskin as a burst of spray showered the cockpit. Her mother was poised to climb for'ard into the darkness. The lifeline was looped neatly over her arm. Yet she hesitated.

'Do you want a torch, Mum?'

'No, it's better without. And I think you'll find it easier without the cabin light on.'

Sam couldn't understand either reasoning, but she decided not to argue. 'Okay.'

'I'll turn it off, okay?'

'Okay.' She waited for the moment of blindness. Before it came, she shut her eyes, then opened them cautiously as she heard her mother climb back into the cockpit. She looked around to reassure herself: south to the white beacon flashing away, south-east to the Tiri light, east. . . She caught her breath. Just emerging from the sea to the north of Tiri Island was a huge globe of soft pink and grey.

'Oh, Mum . . . look,' she breathed. 'A pink moon. Dad said it would be nearly full. Isn't that the most beautiful moon you ever saw?'

Her mother didn't reply, but Sam could see her black figure pause before she left the cockpit. 'Beautiful, Sam.' Her voice faded away. 'I'll enjoy it when I come back . . .' She was gone.

Sam didn't know whether her mother could hear above the sea noises on the foredeck, but she said it anyway: 'Mind where you put your feet, Mum.'

CHAPTER 13

No brandy for Sam

Sam's dark mood returned as she listened intently for the sounds which would reassure her that all was well on the foredeck. Nothing must happen to Mum; nothing must happen to Mum, she kept thinking. She tried to visualize what had to be done; the spinnaker pole had to be unclipped from the mast and manoeuvred into place along the windward deck. The worst part would be lowering it, dangling from the uphaul, in a fore-and-aft line onto the deck.

During a particularly long silence, Sam began to dread that her worst fear was coming true. Something had happened. The pole was too heavy.

'Mum,' she yelled, suddenly panic-stricken. 'You okay?' A faint 'Yes' whipped back with a breaking wave. She sat down, shaking.

A new feeling overwhelmed Sam: a weariness that almost hurt. Hardly surprising, she thought, since it must be getting on for midnight. Sleep would not be possible for hours yet, not until the boat was safely anchored in Bon Accord. That was the most tiring thought of all. Only the moon behind her seemed to offer any comfort. Already it was changing from a dusky pink to pale silver reflected in a wide path across the waves.

She was jolted out of her misery by bumping noises for'ard followed by the movement, half-way along the deck, of a figure crouching by the rail. The shape disappeared behind the dinghy, then eventually made its way along the deck – now faintly rimmed by the rising moon – and climbed slowly into the cockpit.

'The brandy, Sam.'

'Behind you. In the corner.'

'Which corner?'

'By the hatch.'

'Say so.' Sam heard fumbling along the seat in amongst the unused jib sheets; the squeak of a cork being pulled out; then a long outward breath. 'I've been waiting for this.' More fumbling inside the hatch, then a torch beam cut abruptly across the cockpit. 'Ten minutes off midnight. How long was I up there, Sam?'

'I don't know. Long enough. It seemed like hours.'

'That must be,' said Mrs Starr, pausing to take another swig at the bottle, 'the heaviest spinnaker pole in the fleet. It felt more like a flagpole.'

Sam could see enough in the light of the torch to be dismayed by her mother's appearance. Under the black harness, her jumper was saturated with water. Her bare legs were wet and shiny, and trembling violently; her short hair was plastered against her head. If she had been overboard she would hardly have looked wetter and more miserable.

'Have some, Sam. Here.' Sam had never tasted brandy – and she wouldn't on this occasion either. The small bottle slipped through her numbed fingers (or perhaps her mother's fingers, she couldn't tell) and smashed into the cockpit. They both stared down aghast.

'Sam. You idiot! You stupid child.'

'I'm sorry. It slipped. It was wet.'

'All that glass. As if we haven't got enough on our plate. You're always dropping things.'

'I'm not, Mum,' wailed Sam.

'Well, you or one of the others.' She leaned down to pick out the bigger bits of glass from the wooden grating. Sam tried to help.

'I'll do it, Mum. You steer. I'll do it.'

'Now someone's bound to get glass in their feet. With all this water down here, I won't find it all.'

'Let me look too, please, Mum. Please.' She was nearly crying.

'*And* I could have done with some more brandy right now. Not to mention later on in this miserable night . . .'

Sam gave up. She stared out at the sea, trying to concentrate on her job as helmsman-lookout. At least she seemed to be managing that to her mother's satisfaction. But there were no lights near, only the second flashing beacon falling away to the south and a low string of lights marking a town on the coast. They had become separated from the main body of the fleet. Doubly angry – with herself for being so clumsy, and with Mum for being so unfair – she noted through blurred eyes that all the navigation lights were now far away towards the east and north. So much for William's fairyland. She felt cheated.

Apparently satisfied that there were no more splinters of glass to be picked out of the shallow squares of the grating, Mrs Starr sat back with a huge sigh.

'I'm sorry, Mum,' Sam mumbled. She seemed to have been saying sorry all night for things she didn't really believe were her fault.

Her mother nodded a grudging truce. Sam noticed that she was shaking even more than before.

'Aren't you frozen, Mum?' she said anxiously.

'Yes. I'd better change.'

'Mum?' There was a question that had to be asked. They couldn't go sailing on this tack all night, or they'd run aground in the surf at Orewa. 'What are we going to do now?'

Fumbling with the buckle on the harness, Mrs Starr said: 'I read enough of that First Aid book to know we have to get Dad to a doctor, as soon as we can.'

'That's all very well . . .'

'We're half-way, more than half-way to Kawau. At this rate we should be there in, say, an hour.'

'What if he wakes up?'

120

'It won't make any difference. We've got to go on. What else can we do?' In the thin light of the torch, she was coiling up the harness and lifeline. 'We haven't got a radio, so we can't call for help. I thought about turning round and going back to Auckland, but it would mean running before the wind the whole way. I don't fancy the thought of a crash gybe. Besides, the tide would be against us and it would probably take longer than going on to Kawau.'

Sam looked back towards the south, where the city lights loomed very faintly now, above the black finger of the Whangaparaoa peninsula. 'Wouldn't it be quicker if we lowered the mainsail and put the engine on? We wouldn't have to tack then.'

Her mother was lowering herself slowly into the cabin. 'I thought about that too. I know how to get the engine going. The snag is, I just can't shift that gear lever down there. I've tried before, but it needs a stronger arm than mine.'

'Couldn't we try together?' Sam called down. The cabin light flicked on.

'The gap under the seat is only big enough for one arm,' said her mother. 'It's one of the penalties of putting modern things into old boats. Nothing's very easy to work and . . .'

Her voice stopped abruptly. What on earth was she doing, thought Sam. Then once again Mrs Starr came hurtling up the companion-way. From the darkness came the sound of retching. But this time she did not pull herself back into the cockpit; her half-kneeling body suddenly went limp over the coaming. It took Sam a few moments to realize what had happened. She had fainted.

Sam let go the tiller. The boat could go to hell. She leaned down towards the black water, grabbed her mother's shoulders, pulled her head inside the liferails and shook her. 'You can't, Mum, you can't . . .' *Aratika*, without Sam's restraining hand on her helm, rounded up into the wind, so that it seemed Sam's whole world was shaking itself to pieces. Above her the heavy boom thudded to and fro and the mainsail pounded like a drumroll. 'You can't . . . you can't . . .'

Sam couldn't remember what to do when people fainted. Just as she was about to scream down into the cabin to Jane for help, Mrs Starr's shoulders began to twitch. Sam cradled her mother's head across her thighs, watching dismayed as the twitching spread down through her body like an electric shock. Then, as abruptly as it started, the movements stopped. Her eyelids flickered. She looked up blankly at Sam.

'What happened?'

'You fainted.' Sam, numb with fright, stroked her mother's forehead.

'Oh. Oh yes. I suppose I must have. Yes – that ghastly feeling, coming round. Coming back from the dead.'

'You were being sick again.'

Mrs Starr awkwardly tried to pull herself upright. 'I'm sorry, Sam. I've done that once or twice before. Blacked out, I mean, while I'm being sick. I did it once with my head in the toilet.'

'Yuk.' Sam couldn't help a grim smile. 'You gave me an awful fright, Mum.'

'I'm sorry.' If she had been trembling before, Mrs Starr was now shaking so uncontrollably that Sam was afraid she was going to have a fit or faint again.

'Mum, you're frozen. You've got to get those clothes off, somehow.'

'We've got to get to Kawau. Why are we flogging around head to wind?'

'Mum, I'm not doing anything until you've got some dry clothes on. You know how you're always going on at us about keeping warm.'

Mrs Starr didn't reply.

122

'Mum,' said Sam sharply

'I can't go below, Sam. I'll be sick again. And faint again. I don't want to faint again.'

'Well, I'll just have to get them and you'll have to change out here. We can bang about head to wind a bit longer. Anyway, the waves aren't coming in.'

'True.'

Sam was disturbed by the lack of response. 'Come on then. Get those clothes off. Where are your others?'

'I don't know. In my sailing bag?'

Mum, who always knew where everything was! Sam climbed down into the cabin. The smell of damp bodies and wet oilskins seemed to be stronger than ever. No wonder her mother hadn't been able to last more than a few seconds. She did a quick check of the cabin; Jane and Jeremy slept on soundly, and Dad – not a sign of life there either. She preferred not to look at Dad. She grabbed her mother's sailing bag from the quarter berth and hoisted it up into the cockpit.

'There, Mum – get your things.' This was a strange and new feeling and she didn't like it very much; this feeling of dominance over her normally strong mother.

'Where's your oilie? – no, don't answer. I'll find it. Get those wet things off.' Locating the oilie in the usual locker, Sam climbed back into the cockpit and watched her mother begin to pull off her sodden jumper.

'Shorts next. No, do your top half first. T-shirt and bra. They're drenched too.' Her breasts, thought Sam, were no fuller than those of Sam's friends who had grown breasts, yet Mum had three children. And her waist was as slim and firm. 'Here's your dry T-shirt. Jumper.' It was like dressing a child. 'Good. Now your shorts. Underpants too. Take them off.'

'My pants aren't wet.' Even arguing like a child.

'Yes they are. Take them *off*,' said Sam firmly. She held

123

out the dry ones. 'Do you want an extra jumper before you put your oilie on?'

'Yes, please.'

'I'll get one of Dad's. He won't be wanting his for a while.' Climbing below again, she realized how flippant that must have sounded. Obviously Mum was in no mood for jokes; she didn't seem to be in any sort of mood at all. Just switched off. The dry clothes must help. What else could she take up? Some biscuits to settle her stomach? Reminded of stomachs, Sam became aware that the boat's movement in the choppy sea was beginning to have an effect on her too. One of them had to stay fit and able to go below during the rest of the night, so she grabbed the jumper and a packet of wine biscuits from the food locker and rejoined the woebegone person in the cockpit, who was still the skipper, whether she liked it or not.

CHAPTER 14

A question of responsibility

For the first time that night since darkness and disaster had descended on them, Sam and her mother were able to sit side by side in the cockpit and concentrate on sailing the boat. Sam had been able to persuade her mother to take the tiller and get *Aratika* moving again. They were now on port tack, heading back towards the tail end of the fleet and, dark along the horizon, the southern tip of Kawau Island.

But if her mother was feeling better for the dry clothes or the sweetness of the wine biscuits they were both munching, she was not yet ready to say so. Her need seemed to be for silence. Sam knew that she enjoyed helming; more than once she'd heard Dad say that Mum was the best helmsman in the family. It was important now, thought Sam, for her mother to regain her strength from the feeling of *Aratika* under control and going somewhere; anything would be better than that awful wallowing and her mother behaving like a child.

Finishing off her seventh wine biscuit with relish – it might well be the only occasion in her life when she was allowed to tuck into a packet of biscuits without restraint – Sam snuggled closer to her mother. Under the firm black line of the boom, the moon faced her squarely, silvering the tops of the waves. Sam was tempted to put her head on her mother's shoulder and give in to the irresistible urge to sleep. She tried to concentrate on the Tiri light to the south, counting off the fifteen-second intervals between the flashes, but it was no use; her head was too heavy to hold up . . . five flashes, one, twenty-two, two, twenty-two, three, twenty-two . . .

She was on the brink of a cliff, with surf breaking on the rocks below. A hand was holding her back. 'Sam, wake up. Wake *up*.' But the falling feeling persisted, and the sounds of breaking water persisted, even as her eyes flickered open. She must have fallen into the black surf. Then she remembered the cockpit, and *Aratika* driving through the waves, and her mother only just managing to stop her from falling down into the leeward side.

'Sam, I can't hold onto you and the boat at the same time.' The hand was digging into her shoulder. Sam made a valiant effort to sit up.

'I'm sorry, Mum. I couldn't help it. I'm so tired.'

'I know. But we've a long way to go yet.'

The situation seemed to call for an intelligent suggestion. Sam blinked and looked about. The Tiri light hadn't moved since they had resumed sailing; or so it seemed.

'We don't seem to be getting anywhere, Mum. Why don't we put the jib up and go faster?'

'No.' Sam was startled by the emphatic reply.

'Why not?'

'Didn't we decide it would be just another complication? Particularly if we have to go about in a hurry.'

'Yes, but I want to get to Kawau.'

'No!'

'We could manage it, Mum.'

'Not the big genoa, we couldn't. We'd be overcanvassed in this wind.'

'Couldn't you change the jib? I'll steer.'

'Sam, I'm too tired.'

'I could do it then.' Sam regretted her bravado the instant she said it.

'No.'

'What are we going to do then? Flog around out here all night?'

'That's one possibility.'

'What are the others?'

During the long silence that followed, Mrs Starr made a small adjustment to the mainsheet. When she spoke again, her tone had changed; it was light, almost chatty.

'I met a lady recently,' she said. 'At a Christmas party.'

'Yes?'

'She annoyed me. She went on and on about dinghy sailing being the only way to learn to sail. You've got to get out in a dinghy, she said, rig it yourself, race it, make your own decisions. Don't let the men anywhere near, because they never stop telling you what to do.'

'Sounds like a women's libber to me.'

'She might have been. She did have a boatmaster's ticket, I'll say that for her. But I disagreed with her at the time. I said I thought you could learn as much if you sailed a family boat with your husband. You'd get to know your own boat well, and you'd share the responsibility.'

There was another long pause, while Sam's tired brain tried to anticipate her mother's point.

'I'm not so sure she wasn't right, Sam. We've sailed this boat for five summers, a month every Christmas holidays, up and down the Gulf, out to the Barrier, up to the Bay of Islands, down to the Great Mercuries. Yet now I find myself in charge, I feel completely, utterly, totally inadequate.'

Sam, disconcerted, searched around for a reply, for some encouragement that wouldn't sound hollow and silly. She was talking nonsense, of course. Mum knew a lot about sailing. She steered a lot, discussed with Dad which sails to carry, discussed courses, the weather, decisions about where to anchor. Compared with some wives – well, Sam had once heard Dad talking about a woman who refused to take the tiller, refused to touch a rope, refused, even, to buy the stores or help load them on board. She was quite happy to lie around in a bikini while her husband sailed the boat with only the help of their two children who were even younger than the Starrs. Sam had felt sorry for the poor man. It seemed that his wife had all the pleasure and did none of the work.

'What do you think, Sam?' her mother was saying. 'You've sailed the dinghy a lot more than me.'

'Mum, if it was you who'd had the accident and was lying down there, what would Dad do?'

'Put up all the sails and crack on to Kawau. No sweat, he'd say. He knows the way to Kawau like the back of his hand.'

'Why can't we do that? Why won't you let us put up the jib? Dad would.'

After a brief hesitation, Mrs Starr said with quiet intensity, 'Sam, I'm frightened of the boat heeling further. I've got to feel in control.'

'And aren't we?' cried Sam.

'At the moment, yes. But I think the wind's still freshening little by little. I know that jib would be too big. I can't run the risk of a knock-down.'

Sam looked around at the sky with its billions of stars, and the dark shape of Kawau low to the north. 'How can you tell the wind's freshening?'

'There's more weight on the helm. But the main problem is that we just can't follow those boats in the race any more now that we're tacking. We're going to have to do some navigating past all those lights and beacons and rocks ahead. Martello Rock and the others. Dad's never made me navigate. If I got out the compass now, I wouldn't really know what to do with it.' Her voice was still quiet but that steely edge was back.

'Why should Dad think it was always going to be one of you children who fell, never him?' her mother went on remorselessly.

'Mum, we've been through all that.' Sam was too tired for another shouting match.

'They can't stand back, these men, when they get on board a boat. They'll push you aside to winch in a jib if they think they can do it half a second faster with their big strong muscles. Or they'll grab the tiller from you if they think you're pinching. They won't let you pull up the anchor, "protecting" you from hurting your back. Ha! When I think of all the men I know with bad backs!'

'Lisa's mother's got a bad back. Remember meeting her down at Brown's Island on Regatta day?' But Mrs Starr didn't want to know about Lisa's mother.

'And then they complain that women have all the privileges and pleasures of sailing with none of the responsibility.'

Sam stared back at the Tiri light. One, two flashes went by.

'How can you take responsibility if you are never given it?' Mrs Starr said finally.

'Well, Mum, we've got it now.'

'Yes, and I don't like it.'

'But Mum – Dad has the responsibility all the time. Perhaps he finds it heavy too, sometimes.'

'His shoulders are broader. And he's been sailing five times longer than me. Sam, I just don't know what we're going to do between now and sunrise. Four, five hours of dark. Any suggestions? I've said my piece.'

'What are you saying, Mum? We're going to Bon Accord, aren't we? To find a doctor for Dad?' Sam was getting thoroughly confused. She decided you needed to see people's faces as well as hear their voices to find out what they really meant. When her mother didn't reply she went on. 'And anyway, Dad's not like all those men you talk about. He doesn't push you aside or grab the tiller. He says you are better at steering than he is.'

'He's unusual, as I've said before. But I still think he should have given me the opportunity to sail the boat as skipper, for practice. To learn from my mistakes.'

'Why didn't he?'

'We talked about it once or twice.'

'But you never did it.'

Silence.

'But perhaps you didn't want to, all that much,' persisted Sam.

'We just never got round to it.'

'If it wasn't for Dad we wouldn't go sailing at all, would we?' said Sam. 'If you were a solo mother, you wouldn't take us sailing.'

'If I were a solo parent, I couldn't afford it. But no, I wouldn't.'

'But you love sailing. You said so.'

'Yes. But not enough to shoulder the responsibility of taking a family to sea.'

'So you don't want the responsibility, but you're happy enough for Dad to have it. Mum, that's not fair.'

'Yes it is. He was brought up on the boat. He was born with a jib sheet in his hands.'

'Well, if you were brought up on a boat, would you be happy to be a skipper?'

Mrs Starr hesitated. 'You've been sailing since you were seven, Sam. Would you want to own a boat like this and be in charge of it when you are grown up?'

'Oh, I don't know. Yes, why not? If I could afford it, why not?' Despite what all those silly boys at school said about girls – 'You can't sail a boat, you're a girl' – why not indeed. She'd have a good crew. She was beginning to find the conversation tiresome as well as confusing. There was, she felt, some basic flaw in her mother's argument. Tomorrow she would ask Mum more about the responsibility thing, when Dad could join in too. Then she remembered Dad's pale face on the bunk below and the more immediate problem of getting help.

'What *did* you mean,' said Sam, 'saying that you didn't

know what we're going to do next? We're heading for Kawau, aren't we?'

'I'm not sure.'

'Not sure? You've already said we can't go back, and we can't engine, and we can't radio for help.'

'I'm thinking about it.'

Sam licked her salty lips, bewildered at the change in her mother's tone. She cast round in her mind for further intelligent suggestions.

'We're stupid, of course,' she said, after a long silence.

'Why?'

'We could easily have asked for help when those boats came near in the Tiri passage. You know . . . the one we nearly rammed on port – and the others – just after you'd been sick.'

'The first time I couldn't think of anything else other than relief. And I'm not too sure I wanted to give that second guy the satisfaction of being asked.'

'He'd have felt awful if he'd realized.'

'That's his problem. Oh no, he'd have been delighted, taking full charge, doing the big hero rescue bit in the middle of the gulf. Little ladies in distress and all that . . . sacrificing his race in order to . . .'

'Mum, now *you're* being women's libbish!' These abrupt changes of mood and tone were making Sam's head whirl.

'It's not women's libbish, as you say. It's nothing to *do* with women's lib, Sam. To try and cope ourselves without rushing to the nearest man for help? Obviously, if the boat was sinking or Dad was having convulsions, we'd be sending up a flare like anyone else would in the same circumstances. But it isn't, and he isn't. We got through the Tiri passage all right,' she said with a touch of pride; adding, 'by the skin of our teeth, I admit.'

A flare! That was what Sam had been trying to remember for the past half an hour. She knew there was

131

something left they could do. Every New Year's Eve at Kawau, the hundreds of boats anchored there set off flares at midnight, scarlet lightbulbs drifting down on little parachutes, turning the sky red. Illegal, Dad always said; flares were for distress signals, not firework displays. But that didn't stop him enjoying the spectacle as much as the children. If they set off a flare now, lots of boats would come rushing back. And then what? It would be difficult to communicate above the wind and waves. 'What's the trouble?' 'Our skipper has been knocked out.' 'What?' 'Knocked out, our skipper.' 'Who's your first mate, then?' 'My Mum.' 'Who?' 'My *Mum*.' 'You're joking.' 'I'm not.' And they'd all sail about a bit, and one boat might decide to send a man to take over, and the dinghy might get swamped in the rough sea, or he might decide it was simply too rough even to try. Sam concluded that all things considered, it would be easier to get themselves to Kawau. The thought of *Aratika* in a secluded bay, bobbing quietly at anchor, was so beautiful that tears blurred her eyes. To sleep, that was all she wanted.

She stood up and yawned loudly. Another white beacon blinked at her, somewhere east, a long way on the starboard bow. She collapsed down into the leeward seat.

'Mum, you still haven't said what we *can* do,' she wailed. 'What did you mean, saying you're not sure and you're thinking about it? Don't I have any say?'

Just as Sam was beginning to think her plea had fallen on deaf ears, a surprisingly tender voice came from the black silhouette above her.

'You're tired, Sam. We don't have to decide yet. You go below and get half an hour's sleep. I'll be all right for a bit.'

'Are you sure?'

'We can stay on this tack for half an hour, maybe longer. I'll call you if I need help.'

The thought of sleep was overwhelming. To be able to close her gritty eyes and surrender; to lie down flat in the warmth of the cabin. It was too good an offer.

'Okay. Thanks, Mum,' she mumbled, feeling a little shamefaced. She started to haul herself upwards towards the hatch.

'Just find me the chart first, will you? And the torch. I'd better find out where we are and where we're going.'

CHAPTER 15

Shelter!

Down in the cabin Sam could do no more than doze erratically, jerking in and out of consciousness and aware even through her sleep of the water rushing past the hull only a few centimetres from her head. She dreamt of taking part in a swimming race, which turned into her swimming behind *Aratika* through a dark green ocean, trying desperately to catch up; but no matter how hard she stroked, the gap remained the same. Then she was swimming through air, but the wind changed and still she could not close the gap. A great turquoise spinnaker appeared, yet as she looked down she could see there was no one on deck, no one at the tiller, no one controlling the spinnaker as it billowed and fell . . . she stroked through the air faster and faster but *Aratika* was always out of reach and a voice was calling . . .

She was completely awake this time, the dream still vivid. She lay tense for a long moment, frowning up into the blackness of the quarter-berth. Something was different. Did Mum call, did she need help? Something had woken her. She struggled out of the bunk and groped her way upright; what had woken her so abruptly? Breakers on the rocks they were about to crash into? Mum's feeble call for help as she surfaced after falling overboard? The roar of an unbelievable wave bearing down and the helmsman's helpless cry?

She peered up into the cockpit, but there were no signs of impending disaster, only a still figure clearly outlined against the stars and, behind, the sharp line of the backstay with the racing pennant flying bravely. Her mother must have noticed the slight movement inside the hatch.

'You awake, Sam? I didn't call.'

'I head something. Something odd.'

'Like what?'

'I don't know. It woke me up.'

'Human noises? Boat noises? I've checked the chart – there's nothing out here. No boats within cooee. Perhaps you were dreaming. You have funny dreams when you're overtired. Go back to sleep.'

Sam was indeed reluctant to leave the shelter of the cabin unless she had to. She was finding it more difficult to stand upright – a combination, she thought, of *Aratika* heeling more, and her own groggy state. The thought crossed her mind that perhaps she could steer while her mother slept. But her mother sounded steady and in control; Sam decided not to offer. The responsibility was too much anyway: four people's lives dependent on her alone.

She wondered, as she stretched out again, would a boy of her age shrink from that sort of responsibility too? A lot of the boys Sam knew at school were all bluster and talk; but then a boy of twelve would never be told he couldn't do something just because he was a boy. How well you could sail a boat, or anything else for that matter, had nothing to do with what sex you were, thought Sam. Anyone could sail, given the opportunity. It was easy if your family owned a boat; or if you *wanted* to enough, you could join a club and read books and race an Optimist or a P-class – anyone could . . .

Sam had just curled up into an uncomfortable ball when again she found herself alert without knowing why. It was not a noise but a feeling; a feeling that someone in the cabin wanted something. Then she heard a groan above the water noises. A deep, man's groan. She was so used to the idea of Dad being tucked up on the leeward bunk, out of action, that it took her a few moments to realize that he might be coming round. More quickly this time, she struggled upright.

'Mum,' she called as her fingers fumbled for the light. 'I know what it was. Dad, making a noise.'

'You'd better have a look at him. Put the cabin light on.'

'I *am*.' Her hand found the small metal lever. With her eyes so used to darkness, she had to turn away from the sudden glare. She felt her way for'ard and leant right over the table to pull back the blanket. Jane was fast asleep, and Dad . . .? Under her reluctant hand his forehead felt as damp and cold as it had up on the deck. And there was no change in his appearance that she could see in the shadows, no movement under the eyelids. She sat down on the edge of the bunk opposite and braced herself, prepared to watch and listen for a few minutes. She wondered how long she could sit without sliding off into sleep again. The first waves of drowziness were not long in coming; she roused herself, took a second look at Dad to check that she could report nothing positive, and staggered to the hatchway.

'Well?' said her mother, impatient.

'He looks just the same, but I'm sure I heard something before,' said Sam, relieved to feel the cool air on her forehead.

'Do you think he's coming round?'

'Yes and no.'

'That's as clear as mud.'

Sam was so tired she couldn't think. 'He looks just the same. Dead as a dodo.'

'Sam, please . . .'

'All right, all right. Can I go back on the bunk? I'll stay awake and listen.'

'No, you wouldn't.'

'I've hardly been asleep at *all*,' said Sam, provoked to indignation. 'How long have I been asleep? Ten minutes, I bet!'

'Over half an hour. Getting on for an hour, actually.

Sam, you've got to look after Dad if and when he wakes up. I can't go below, you know that.'

Sam rested her head against the companion-way. The night would never end; her father would never wake up; the Tiri light would always be on the horizon; Kawau was a mythical island that didn't exist; *Aratika* was a boat doomed to sail on for ever and ever; and her mother was a seasick skipper who could never go below. There was no hope. All she wanted to do was sleep. She wondered if it were possible to sleep standing up. Would her body, braced against the sloping ladder, allow her aching head to go to sleep, just by itself?

'Sam. Sam! Come quick. It's Dad.' Jane's voice cut across her misery. She turned. Jane was trying, with considerable difficulty, to fight her way out of the bunk. 'Dad's twitching all over and making groaning noises. Get Mum.'

'I can't get Mum,' said Sam flatly.

'Why not?'

'She's steering. And besides . . . oh, never mind.' There was no point in telling Jane of Mum's seasickness. Thank goodness she had slept through all that. Sam groped her way past Jane to the bunk. She had been right; there were her father's eyes open and looking straight at her. She could have wept with relief.

'Dad. Oh, Dad, you're alive,' she cried, stretching out to touch his bristly grey cheek. But there was no response, no answering smile. Didn't he recognize her? 'Dad. You're all right.'

'Give him time,' said Jane's loud voice. Together they stared down, willing him to smile back, however faintly.

'Dad?' There was a slight flicker in his eyes, and then, quite suddenly, he turned his head to one side in an ineffectual attempt to sit up. For the third time that night Sam heard and saw the preliminary warnings of someone about to vomit. He couldn't – not in here, all over the blankets and the carpet! Jane was nearer to the galley. 'A basin, quick, Jane. He's going to be sick.'

Jane reacted quickly, grabbing a container from just inside the locker, but she was not quite in time. Better than nothing, thought Sam as she tried, without much success, to lift her father's head. The table was getting in the way.

'I need some towels,' she called, aware that her younger sister was lingering near the hatch away from the smell. It was about time she did something she didn't want to do.

'Where do I get towels from?'

'Your bag, my bag, anyone's bag,' said Sam irritably. 'The spare ones from the locker up there above Jeremy.' She waved vaguely in the direction of the locker behind her, not daring to take her eyes off her father's face. It had been a couple of minutes now since his last long spasm. He lay there, eyes closed again, his jaw trembling. She pulled the unsoiled blanket up over the damp jumper and used the first of Jane's towels to wipe his forehead and mouth. Did people go unconscious again, just like that, or had he fallen asleep, she wondered apprehensively.

'Here, take this,' she said to Jane, holding out the basin.

'You don't expect me to . . .?'

'Yes, I do,' snapped Sam. 'Over the side. Don't spill it.' Who did Jane think she was?

She searched her father's face for any signs; he seemed to have drifted back to sleep. Trying hard not to breathe too deeply, nor think too closely about the job she had to do, she finished the wiping up and made a bundle of the towels and soiled top blanket. She had never seen an adult being sick before – except Mum, and she always managed to do it discreetly over the lee rail. The smell, strong and sour, was beginning to worry her. She supposed the best thing was to take the whole messy bundle outside and get some fresh air.

'What shall I do with these?' she said wearily, climbing out into the cockpit.

'Put them in the locker under the seat,' said Mrs Starr. 'Jane, help her.' Typically, Jane didn't exactly spring to help, noted Sam. She put the cover back into place and sat down on it.

'Well, what's the story, Sam?' inquired Mrs Starr in her I-shouldn't-have-to-ask voice.

'Dad's sort of sleeping.'

'What do you mean, sort of?'

'Well, when he finished being sick he sort of drifted off again. Sleeping or unconscious like he was before, I don't know. How do you tell the difference?' She noticed that the moon was now well up in the sky. In other circumstances she would be thinking that a moon at sea was one of the most beautiful things she had ever seen.

'I honestly don't know,' her mother was saying.

'Don't know what?'

'What's the matter with you, Sam?' her mother said sharply. 'Are you feeling sick?' But before Sam could reply, Jane spoke.

'If he's only sleeping then you should be able to wake him up.'

There was another long pause.

'You might be right,' said Mrs Starr finally. 'Sam, can you take the tiller?'

'Why?'

'I've got to take a quick look at Dad, even if it makes me sick in the process.'

Sam caught her breath. 'Mum, no – you might faint again.'

'Faint again?' said Jane. She didn't miss a beat, thought Sam. 'What do you mean, faint again?'

'She fainted. While you were asleep,' said Sam. Of all the bad moments that night, Mum's fainting had been one

139

of the worst. She couldn't bear the thought of it happening again.

'I only blacked out for a few seconds, Jane,' Mrs Starr said hastily. 'If I start to feel bad I'll come up, I promise. Sam, you take over. You *are* okay, I suppose?'

'I suppose so,' said Sam, slowly hauling herself up to the windward seat. All her old fears of being alone at the tiller came crowding back. She could feel the increased pressure on the helm and the stronger wind against her face. Grandmother's weather. She pulled her oilskin hood up just before a wave broke over the cockpit.

Her mother went carefully down the ladder and made her way for'ard to the starboard bunk. She leant over and shook Dad's shoulder; she seemed to be talking and waiting; then she was standing, moving swiftly towards the cockpit, one hand over her mouth, up the companion-way and down over the lee rail.

'Jane, hold her!' cried Sam. It was going to happen again, the retching, the blackout, the convulsive jerks and twitches as she came round. They waited silently for her to recover. Looking at them both sitting slumped in the lee seat, Sam could see that Jane was as frightened as she herself had been earlier.

'I'm okay,' mumbled Mrs Starr. She spat on the deck. 'I'm okay.'

'You're not,' said Jane. 'You're shaking all over like a leaf.' Her voice was blunt, but she looked up with the same doubt and fear that Sam was feeling once more. Without Mum, what would happen to them?

'It'll pass.' Mrs Starr leant back against the coaming. A minute, maybe two minutes passed.

'I think,' began Mrs Starr, taking deep deliberate breaths, 'I think Dad . . . is awake. He mumbled something . . . about getting the spinnaker off . . . and then . . . he seemed to go back to sleep. He's not breathing as fast.'

Again they waited while she spat into the water.

'Then . . . he woke up . . . and said something about coming up on watch.'

'He sounds a bit confused,' said Jane. 'Thinks he's still in the Navy, probably.'

'Jane, how can you joke at . . .'

'She's probably right, Sam,' said Mrs Starr flatly, her voice stronger now. 'I said I'd call him when it was time, and he seemed to think that was okay because he turned on his side, like he does at home, and settled down. I had the feeling it was a proper sleep.' She rubbed her eyes with her hands. 'Lucky him.'

'What's the time?' said Jane.

'I don't know. Late. Too late.' She sat for a moment with her head in her hands. 'The smell down there is appalling.'

'It was worse before,' said Sam. It occurred to her that there had been no thanks for dealing with the mess below. Typical. And she still couldn't see why her mother had insisted on running the risk of putting herself out of action simply to see what Dad looked like. It was almost as if she didn't trust anyone.

'If you think Dad has gone to sleep, what difference does that make?'

'Difference to what?'

'To what we decide to do.'

'Not much. We haven't got much choice, have we?'

'Where are we anyway?' said Jane. 'And what's happened to the rest of the boats in the race?'

'They've all gone up through the channel, over there,' said Mrs Starr, pointing northwards over the port bow. 'Those white stern lights, see? I suppose most of them are anchored by now.'

'How come we got so far behind?' asked Jane.

'Various reasons,' said Mrs Starr after a short pause.

She made a move to pull herself up to the windward seat alongside Sam. 'I'll take over now, Sam.'

'Do you feel all right, Mum?'

'Yes.' They swapped places. Sam was only too pleased to hand over the tiller. 'Thanks, Sam. You did well.'

Sam didn't reply.

'How long before we get up to Bon Accord, Mum?' said Jane. 'I'm dying to go to bed properly.'

'We're not going to Bon Accord.' There was a new note in her voice.

'What?' said Sam, incredulous.

'We all need sleep, Sam.'

'But . . .'

'I know. We still need a doctor, but I think we can wait until morning.'

'What are we going to do then? Flog around out here for the rest of the night?'

'No. We need shelter and sleep. There's Bosanquet Bay,' she said, pointing to the black hump of Kawau ahead. 'We're going to put in there instead.'

CHAPTER 16

Bosanquet Bay

It seemed like a betrayal. Their course that night, from the very moment that Sam had heard about such a thing as a night race to Kawau, had been set for Bon Accord and the rewards of lying peacefully at anchor in Mansion House Bay. All the problems they had faced together had got them this far, two-thirds of the way. Yet here was her mother changing her mind and deciding to run for shelter. Sam was piqued that she hadn't shared in making the decision or at least been asked what she thought. Another adult unilateral decision.

'Why, Mum?' she said sullenly. 'It's not all that far to Mansion House.'

'Where's Bosanquet, Mum?' Jane sounded so accepting that Sam would have hit her if she could have done so without toppling down into the lee seat.

'Dead ahead,' said Mrs Starr. 'It's that bay we went into last summer, remember?' No, I don't, thought Sam, craning her neck to scan without enthusiasm the black rim of the island rising directly ahead of *Aratika*.

'Why can't we just go on?' persisted Sam. 'You've been looking at the chart. You said it wasn't all that far *hours* ago.'

'I've looked at the chart all right. After that beacon over there' – she pointed with her left hand almost abeam to a flashing white light seen intermittently through the spray – 'is the Beehive, and Passage Reef and a couple of other reefs and Martello Rock thrown in for good measure. And you know how flukey the wind always is in Bon Accord.'

'Sounds interesting,' said Jane.

'That's one way of putting it.'

'But what about Dad?' cried Sam. 'What about the doctor?'

'Sam, don't you understand? I can't risk it, don't you see?'

'No, I don't see. Didn't you say Dad would crack on to Kawau, no sweat, if it was you down there! Why can't we?'

'Sam, don't back me up against a wall.' It was a plea, not an order, and her voice was shrill. 'I only know I can't take *Aratika* through that channel at low tide with visibility lousy and the wind on the nose.' She paused to let her words sink in, and then continued in a more controlled voice, 'At Bosanquet it'll be sheltered and we can all get some rest.'

'But Dad needs a doctor, you said so yourself. We won't find one in Bosanquet. There's nothing in Bosanquet.'

There was an ominous silence.

'That's where you and Jane come in. At first light I want you to walk over the hill to Mansion House and get help.'

Sam, defeated, had no more to say. She wasn't walking anywhere if she could help it. The night had been one long conflict. Mum could look after Dad from now on; all she wanted to do was sleep . . . sleep. There was something funny about Bosanquet, but she couldn't remember . . . She drew herself in like a snail going into its shell, her head between her knees and her back tucked into the corner of the cockpit, and wept.

Dimly, over the sounds of the wind in the rigging and the slap of the bow driving through the waves, she heard her mother tell Jane to go below and stay with Dad and some protest from Jane about the smell, followed by a terse reply: something about needing Sam on deck and taking her gently because she'd had a hard time, 'and don't ask me to elaborate, Jane, because I'm not going to,' in a voice as firm as concrete.

Sam didn't care if they knew she was crying. Eventually when she raised her head, it was to discover that Jane had disappeared as requested and the cabin light was off once again. Now she could cry as much as she liked, as long as she couldn't be heard above the hiss of the waves and the wind.

Mum must have known, thought Sam bitterly, that she wouldn't face going on to Bon Accord when it really came to the point. All that brave talk about responsibility. That must have been why she let me go off and have a sleep, she thought: soften me up for a beastly walk over a beastly hill. Yet even through her disappointment, Sam knew that changing your mind required its own sort of courage. And who knew what was best out here in the middle of the night in the middle of the ocean, with everyone so dead beat they could hardly sit up? She supposed that it was Dad's waking up, apparently not so badly injured, that had tipped the scales in favour of Bosanquet. What was it about that bay she remembered from their visit last summer? Something they had looked for . . .

Sam almost wished that Dad had got a little bit worse, just bad enough for them to send up a flare. One of those white stern lights disappearing into the night would have an alert crew member looking backwards just as their red call for help zoomed up into the sky. Then they could hand over the burden . . . and sleep.

Her eyelids were hot, throbbing and gritty. She was tired of trying to stay upright on the windward seat, braced rigid, so she flopped down onto the other side of the cockpit. Stretching down with her fingertips to touch the foam swirling past the hull, she found the water warm on her fingers and the pressure against her hand strangely soothing.

She was startled by a cry from above.

'Sam?'

What now? She looked up at the black figure of her mother.

'Sam, are you being sick?'

'Of course not.'

'What are you doing?'

'Just feeling the water. I'm bored and I'm so tired I could drop. We've been sailing all night and I'm sick of sailing. How far is it to Bosanquet, anyway?'

'It's about . . . there.' Her mother stretched a black arm vaguely towards the dark hulk of the island. 'I'd guess about two kilometres, or so. We'll have to put in a couple of boards. Come up here and have a look.'

Sam hauled her way up to sit alongside her mother, close enough for their outstretched thighs, sticky with salt water, to press together. A hand as cold and wet as hers came over and sought a reassuring grip. 'I think it's that greyish strip you can see in there,' said Mrs Starr quietly after a long silence. 'Just to the left of the highest point of the island, see?'

'No.' She knew she sounded like a pouting little toddler but she couldn't help it. For once, her mother did not pursue the point but left her to search the coastline that was looming slowly closer like some monstrous black wave. How could she be expected to see anything, now that the moon was veiled by high patchy clouds? It was not even possible to tell where the sea broke against the shoreline and where the land started. Yet after a minute or two, as her eyes became accustomed to reading the subtle differences of tone between various greys and a blackness so dense that it seemed to go on for ever, she could just make out a definite paler strip among the jagged shapes at sea level. It looked craggy and forbidding, nothing like an inviting place to anchor a boat in pitch darkness.

'We're going in there?' she asked.

The grip on her hand tightened. 'Yes.' Shortly after,

Mrs Starr withdrew her hand and Sam was aware of her scuffling around inside her oilskin pouch and producing an untidily-folded chart.

'The torch, in the usual place, please Sam?' she asked, her voice giving nothing away. She began to examine the chart with the same remote air, making no move to share the yellow beam of light or whatever information she was gleaning. Sam felt excluded, first from the decision to go into Bosanquet, and now from any consideration of just how they were going to get into the bay without hitting a rock. Hadn't she earned more than that from her mother on this miserable and never-ending night?

'Can I steer for you, while you look at the chart?' she offered.

'It's all right.'

That's it Mum, thought Sam. You can get into Bosanquet all by yourself, if that's the way you want it. She jumped down into the lee seat again, leaving her mother peering at her stupid chart. A nice big wave broke against the hull, sending its spray right over the cockpit, right over Mum. Oh dear, thought Sam unkindly, Mum's getting Dad's precious chart wet, that he always keeps in plastic folders and insists on being folded correctly. Against the pearly black sky, she could see her mother shaking the water off it.

The torch was turned off. Time passed. They sailed on for maybe twenty minutes or more without speaking. The night, it seemed to Sam, was getting darker and darker. She was drifting off to sleep again when she heard a terse 'Ready about.' But there was nothing to do, with no jib sheets to winch in and Mrs Starr apparently not wanting help with the backstays. Surprisingly, she didn't ask Sam to warn Jane, assuming of course that Jane was even awake. It was almost as if she'd forgotten about the others and about Sam too. Glumly, through eyes heavy with sleep, Sam noted the white beacon dropping astern.

'Ready about,' again, and they were back on port tack with the flashing white light now directly astern and *Aratika* headed for the shadowy strip her mother had identified as Bosanquet. They were getting too close for any chance of sleep. From her downhill perch, Sam could see on the starboard bow that a group of tall black rocks, one or two big enough to be islands, had detached themselves from the land and stood proud against the horizon.

'Sam?' It was her mother at her most bossy. Slowly Sam unwound her arms from around her frozen legs and tried to straighten her back.

'You awake and ready?'

'Sort of.'

'How much sort of? I can't see how much, can I?'

'I'm awake.'

The torch flashed on again for another check of the chart and then at Sam, presumably to reassure Mrs Starr that Sam was in a fit state to do whatever was needed.

'Don't shine that in my eyes, Mum.'

'When we get into the bay, Sam, we've got two things to do: get the anchor down and get the mainsail down, in that order. Once we get in the lee of the wind it should be quite peaceful, but one thing we mustn't do is to find ourselves without steerage way. We've no engine.' Her voice was surprisingly alert, thought Sam with grudging admiration, considering all that had gone before. Sam pulled herself up onto the windward seat, to show some sort of co-operation. She was shivering again, partly from cold, partly from fear, with a prickle of foreboding crawling up and down her spine. The black-on-black crags along the coastline ahead seemed to be waiting for them.

'Have we been in here before?' she asked.

'Yes, just before New Year, remember, on our way to Mansion House. It's a deep horse-shoe bay, with a nice beach. We had a barbecue there. And then went for a walk to . . .'

She stopped abruptly.

'To what?'

'To . . . admire the view.' But that's not what you were originally going to say, thought Sam. What had we gone there for, some sort of treasure hunt . . . ? But her mother wasn't leaving time for remembering. 'The chart says there's ten metres of water just inside the line between the two headlands. That's at low tide, I presume.'

'What time is low tide?'

'About an hour ago, around two.'

It was three in the morning? Sam had lost all track of time.

'We'll try and anchor just when we see we're level with the two points. That should give us plenty of water, maybe too much, but we could drift in a bit later with the incoming tide.'

She's certainly worked it all out, admitted Sam. Her own mind was still trying to remember what it was they had gone to see or find on that picnic.

'I want you to go into the forepeak, Sam, with the torch, and get the anchor out on deck. It's not going to be easy, under all that spinnaker.' She was holding out the torch.

Sam started to say, 'Couldn't you . . .' but realized the futility of her question. It was not possible for her mother to go into the heaving forepeak to get the anchor. She gave a huge sigh which went all the way down to the tips of her numb toes.

'Don't complain, Sam,' said Mrs Starr tersely. 'You know I can't . . .'

'Yes, I know, I *know*. I'm going.'

She decided she couldn't face the smell in the cabin, so she began a slow-motion climb along the windward deck.

Pausing by the shrouds while *Aratika* rose and fell to a series of big waves, Sam remembered she was without a lifeline, so she sat down and crawled the rest of the way. Awkwardly she untied the lashing of the canvas cover and prised open the hatch.

As she lowered her legs down into the square hole, she came into contact with a slimy sea of cold wet terylene. It seemed to cling to her bare legs like seaweed. She wished she had decided to go through the cabin; at least she could have pushed aside this clammy forest before she entered it. She was relieved to flick on the torch and reassure herself that it was only a sail!

She propped the torch on top of the bunk where Jeremy usually slept and began to scoop armfuls of the spinnaker onto the other bunk. Bent double, her stomach heaving to the rhythmic rise and fall of the musty triangular cave of the bow, Sam knew she would have to be quick. The torch fell to the sloping floor and went out. She groped with outstretched fingers and felt the rubber tube of the torch and the hard metal stock of the anchor simultaneously. She shook the torch in desperation and was rewarded with a flickering light. There was the anchor, its chain and warp heaped nearby. Grasping the anchor with both hands, she was just able to lift it up onto the bunk. Then she had to stand up and poke her head through the hatch to get a breath of fresh air. Dead ahead rose the black edge of the hills above Bosanquet; she was shocked to see how close it looked – the length of their beach at home perhaps, maybe less. Why hadn't they got the anchor up earlier? They had left it all too late.

'Sam. Hurry up.' The voice from the helm was agitated.

'I *am*.'

She threaded her top half back down through the narrow hole and looked at the anchor. How could she lift it up through the hole? She doubted she could lift it above her head. There was only one other way: she climbed out again, lay down flat on the deck and leaned over, reaching down inside. Her arms weren't quite long enough, so she had to wriggle forward until her head was hanging down inside too. Then she could just reach the bunk to grab the anchor and, with every bit of her fading strength, she lifted it up through the hatch. It wasn't the weight of the anchor itself – she'd lifted it before and knew it wasn't very heavy – but the long length of chain wrapped around the stock. With a final effort, she lifted the anchor clear of the hatch and dumped it heavily on the deck. She was gasping as she pushed herself up into a sitting position.

'Sam?'

'It's up on deck,' she yelled.

'Good. Put it on the windward side, up against something so it can't roll off, and wrap some chain around the bollard,' came the faint reply. 'Then come back here.'

She was too tired to feel any great satisfaction as she climbed back towards the cockpit.

'Got the torch, Sam?'

'I left it on the bunk.'

'Doesn't matter. I'll get it. Now listen, Sam,' she said urgently, 'I'm going up to get the anchor warp ready. You're going to take the helm.'

'Mum, please . . .'

'Sam, you've got to. Look, I've been going over this in my mind for the last two hours. You can't do the anchor. Any minute now we're going to get into the lee of the headland there. We'll stop all this heeling and pitching about. You've only got to keep her going, just as she is. And you'll be able to hear me quite clearly once we're out of the wind.'

'Why can't I drop the anchor?'

'It's too heavy for you. Now look . . .' and even as she spoke *Aratika* gave one last dipping salute to the northerly and straightened up. Her movement changed to a smooth forward glide; her bowsprit steadied. In the deep silence, Sam could hear the rustle of the bush behind the beach, the hiss of the wake, and a long rising 'weeeeek' which she knew to be a weka.

'Thank God for that,' said Mrs Starr, her voice over-loud and hollow against the hills, like someone talking across the wooden boards of an empty school hall. Sam said nothing; no words could express her relief at being able to stand upright again.

'I'm going for'ard. You take her, Sam. Keep her pointing exactly as she is. We've got a fair amount of way on, but I haven't got long.'

Sniffing, Sam moved to take over at the tiller. The wood was warm and moist from her mother's grasp.

'Let the mainsheet out, just a bit,' came the voice from the foredeck, followed by the metallic rattle of the anchor chain reverberating through the boat. Sam looked anxiously into the blackness of the cabin; surely the noise was loud enough to wake at least one of the three below. Sure enough, a ghostly face appeared in the hatchway.

'What's going on?' Jane's voice. 'I heard a whole lot of clunking.'

'Tell you later,' said Sam brusquely.

'Tell me now.'

'I can't.' Sam was concentrating on trying to lift the mainsheet out of its cleat where it had been held fast most of the night. At last it jerked free and she was able to ease the sheet through the heavy wooden block.

'How much, Mum?' she called, ignoring Jane.

'Only a bit. Whatever you think. Enough to catch any little puff that's around.'

Sam watched the boom swing outwards, then she jammed the sheet home again into the cleat.

'Where on earth are we?' said Jane, climbing out into the cockpit and gazing around at the dark hills now almost enclosing them, the tall craggy islands standing guard at the eastern end. 'Why are you steering, Sam? Where's Mum?'

'Will you shut up, Jane? We're anchoring. I've got to be able to hear Mum.' *Aratika* was still slipping smoothly towards the grey line of the beach. They would have to drop the pick soon. It would be a matter of a minute, maybe less, before they came into line with the two inner arms of the bay where Mum had said they should anchor.

The answer, when it came precious seconds and more rattling noises later, confirmed her suspicions. Something had got fouled up. Mum wasn't ready.

'Bear away, bear away.'

'What do you mean?' wailed Sam.

'Pull the tiller towards you. Hard,' yelled Mrs Starr. Sam pulled frantically until she jammed herself right back into the corner of the cockpit, with the tiller over as far as it could go. *Aratika* slewed off to starboard, the boom and mainsheet traveller clattering, until she was pointing out to sea again.

'What's she doing? What's going on?' asked Jane.

'Jane, be quiet . . .'

'Head her out to sea . . .'

'Mum, what's the matter . . .?'

'Pull the tiller back amidships, Sam. We don't want to go round in a circle.'

'I have,' said Sam, confused. 'Mum, what's happening?'

'The anchor warp's caught below in all that messed-up spinnaker. I'm just going down to clear it.' Her agitated voice floated faintly up from the cabin as she dropped down into the forepeak. 'Head her out to sea.'

I can't stand it, thought Sam, that fresh northerly again. There was no way of telling how far they could drift before losing the shelter of the land and picking up the wind again. Sam felt they were slipping out of the peaceful embrace of the bay. Yet even as she waited for the next

153

instruction from the foredeck, she could tell that *Aratika* had all but lost steerage way and was bobbing quietly to the small swell rolling into the beach. Fearfully she looked up at the high cliff over to their right, how far away she couldn't tell. Which way would the tide carry a helpless yacht? Dad, she cried silently, wake up . . . help us . . .

'Okay. Now put the helm over again. Away from you,' came the call. Sam did, but there was no responding swing from the bowsprit.

'I said put the helm over.'

'I have,' Sam called. 'She won't answer.'

'*Hard* over?'

'Yes, as far as it'll go.'

Mrs Starr appeared on the foredeck, erect as a figurehead. The tension in that black silhouette was so great that Sam felt like screaming. Even Jane had fallen silent.

Sam saw her mother move towards the bowsprit and bend down to take the weight of the anchor. The chain clanked along the deck behind her.

'We'll just have to anchor here, then.'

There was a splash followed by the sound of the chain grinding down through the brass fairlead, and then silence as the long rope snaked its way towards the bed of the sea.

CHAPTER 17

An apology

After the night's constant turmoil, the stillness was so overwhelming that Sam sat down and began to cry. She made no effort to stifle her sobs; she didn't care who heard her now, Jane, Mum or anyone. They had anchored the boat and that, for the moment, was enough. With eyes full of hot tears, she turned and surveyed the coastline's black arms: a high promontory, then the grey strip of the beach, more rocks and finally the craggy islands at the eastern end.

Jane had put a comforting arm around her shoulders. They shared the silence as Sam's tears ebbed.

'Sam, we're here, we're all right.'

'I know, but . . .' She buried her head against Jane's shoulder. 'I just want to go to sleep.'

'I wish the sun would come up. I don't like the dark.'

'What's the matter, Sam?' They both looked up at the figure busy by the forestay, apparently securing the anchor. 'You hurt?' called Mrs Starr.

'No.'

'Okay then.' Sam had heard that tone before: brisk and unsympathetic. 'I'm letting the main halyard go. Will you two help me stow the main?'

Sam sniffed hard as she wiped eyes and nose on her oilskin sleeve.

'Come on, Sam,' said Jane, sighing. 'Mum wants help.'

'She's been saying that all night.'

'Stop grizzling, Sam.' As she spoke, Mrs Starr let go the halyard, so that the mainsail began its precipitous descent to the cabin top with a noisy clatter of wire. Sam and Jane instinctively put up their arms to protect themselves.

'Get the sail ties, Jane. They should be on the chart table. Sam, the crutch for the boom.'

In silence, the two children and their mother bundled the big sail into an untidy sausage along the boom. Sam knew that the job was below Dad's standard, which demanded that the mainsail be smooth and tight, no ends hanging loose, but nothing mattered any more as long as it was out of the way. Now she could sleep.

'Jane, I want you to go below and check Dad. Sam, come up here and hold the torch.'

'What else do we have to do, Mum?' asked Sam sullenly. 'Can't we sleep now?'

'We've got to get the dinghy off. You hold the torch while I untie the lashings.'

'Why? We're not going ashore yet. Why can't we wait until it gets light?' At the back of Sam's mind was the hope that by daybreak Dad would be awake and sufficiently recovered for them to sail to Bon Accord. 'I'm so tired, Mum.'

'You're not the only one. I'm not too happy about anchoring out here. We're further out than I intended, but . . . well, we might have to tow the boat in with the dinghy. It's the only way we've got of moving around, with the engine out of action and not a breath of wind in here.'

'I though you said you could remember how to work the engine?'

'Yes, but I can't get it into gear, remember? It apparently never occurred to either William or your father that one day someone less strong than themselves might have to work it. A woman, even.'

'Have you really tried?'

'I have, Sam,' said Mrs Starr testily, 'and that's when I've been awake and fit, not dog-tired and frozen like I am now. It's a pig of a thing. Here, hold the torch still.' Sam tried to steady the beam over her mother's wet fingers fumbling with Dad's firm navy-style knots. 'Is that the last one? Can you see any more?'

Sam ran the torch over the varnished wood, wondering how they were to get the heavy dinghy turned over and lowered into the water. It would be a difficult enough job even with Dad in charge.

'I don't think we're strong enough,' grumbled Sam. How are we going to lift it without Dad?'

'Without Dad? What do you mean, without Dad?' said a male voice behind her. Sam spun around, her heart pounding in her throat with the biggest fright of her life. Against the black hills she could see nothing, not even the faintest outline, but she knew he must be standing there, in the cockpit, watching their silhouettes against the sky. 'What are you two doing up?'

'Dad! Oh, Dad, you *are* alive.' Her only thought was to rush into the cockpit and give him the mightiest bear-hug her tired arms could squeeze. 'Dad . . . you're all right . . .' She clambered over the winch and up against the tall figure by the hatchway, throwing her arms up where she thought his neck would be. His bristly chin prickled against her cheek.

'What's all this? Of course I'm all right. Why shouldn't I be?' His hand was ruffling her damp hair. 'What have I done to deserve this?'

Jane's voice sounded close by, apologetic and upset, as she pushed past them both into the cockpit. 'Mum, I tried to get him to stay on his bunk, but he wanted to know what you were doing on deck in the middle of the night.'

'And why should I stay on my bunk?' said Mr Starr. 'What are you doing up here, Mum? Are we dragging the anchor?'

'No, nothing's wrong,' said Mrs Starr in a voice as smooth as oil.

'Well, why are you awake? And Sam too?'

With only the slightest of hesitations, Mrs Starr replied. 'Having a pee.'

Sam heard Jane beside her snort, and turn the snort into a cough.

'What an odd place to have a pee,' said her father mildly. 'You usually use the bucket in the cockpit.'

'First I used the bucket. Then I thought I'd come up and look at the stars. I'm sitting here enjoying the beauty of the night . . .' Her voice trailed off unconvincingly.

Sam, her cheek flat against the damp wool of her father's jumper and still basking in the protection of his strong arms around her, wondered who would make the next move in this bizarre game. For some reason, her father's reappearance on the scene seemed to have quite nonplussed her mother. It was almost as though she were playing for time.

'It's a funny thing,' her father began, sounding puzzled, 'you say you are sitting when I can see quite clearly that you are standing.'

Only now did Mrs Starr move deliberately towards the cockpit.

'Nick, why don't you . . .?'

'Now why should you say one thing when . . .?'

'It doesn't matter what I'm doing. Come back . . .'

'I don't understand what we're all doing up.'

'I told you . . . having a pee.'

'I must have been very tired. I've got such a headache.'

'Hardly surprising,' Jane began, 'after . . .' But Mr Starr was now talking to himself and didn't hear her.

'I can't remember coming in here, you know that? Nice sheltered place, Drunks.'

Drunks? thought Sam. Drunks was the yachties' name for Islington Bay, between Rangitoto and Motutapu; they had anchored there only last weekend, the night before the Anniversary Regatta. She was beginning to understand. He thought he was in Drunks!

Jane was first off the mark. 'Dad, this isn't . . .' but her words triggered at last a decisive reaction from their mother.

'Jane, be quiet. I think we should all go back to bed.' She climbed onto the seat. 'Off you go, the cockpit's not big enough for all of us roaming around.'

'I don't understand why I've got this jumper on,' Sam heard her father's bewildered voice go on. 'I don't usually sleep in a jumper. It must have been cold. Are we expecting the anchor to drag, Mum? I'd better check the anchor . . .'

'I've done that, Nick.'

'Perhaps I'd better have a look . . .'

'No, it's all right.'

'Help me get this jumper off, Mum. It smells funny.'

'Sure . . . when Jane has done as she's told.'

'Which bunk, Mum?' asked Jane.

'Which bunk, she says,' said Mr Starr. 'What a child. Your own bunk, of course.'

'I can't go there. Mum, won't you be wanting the quarter-berth?' Jane, undeterred, was still blocking the hatchway.

'Why can't you, and why would Mum be wanting the quarter-berth?' Sam heard her father grunting as he struggled with the damp jumper. The cockpit was becoming very crowded.

'Well, she can't sleep anywhere else, can she? Jeremy's on the port bunk and the front cabin is all full of wet spinnaker because you . . .'

'Jane,' came Mrs Starr's despairing cry. 'Will you get down on that quarter-berth and go to sleep?'

'Why the quarter-berth? That's Sam's place, isn't it?' said Mr Starr. It was getting too much for Sam, torn between a desire to laugh at this circular argument about bunks and pity for her poor father who was obviously hopelessly confused and in no state to sort out anything.

159

And Jane, also confused, hadn't realized that something was still wrong with Dad even though he was awake and talking.

'Don't worry. I'll fix the kids.' Her mother spoke gently but firmly. 'Come on now. Get back to sleep, Nick.'

'I'm very thirsty,' he mumbled. 'There's a foul taste in my mouth.'

'I'll get you a drink of water. Come on.'

Their voices became an indistinct murmur as Mum succeeded in persuading him back onto the bunk, covered him with blankets, and then sat with him while he dropped back to sleep. She wouldn't put the cabin light on, that would only reveal the evidence of a hard night – wet clothes and towels lying around, the First Aid kit open and untidy, and not one of them, even Jeremy, actually in pyjamas.

Left alone in the cockpit, Sam felt desolate. She pulled her knees up against her chest and tried to find a comfortable rest for her back against the hard edges of cleats and coamings. Her yearning for sleep was now so complete that she knew if she lay down on the wooden seat she would drop straight off, with tangled ropes for her pillow and the cool night air for her blanket. Her head dropped onto her knees. There was nothing to do and no bunks left. The front cabin where Jane and Jeremy normally slept was full of spinnaker. Perhaps she should make a final effort and stagger along to the for'ard hatch and drop down onto it; slimy as it was, it would at least be softer than this wooden seat . . .

What would Mum do, once she had got Dad back to sleep? There was no bunk for her either, unless she moved Jeremy again. They would have to share. Well, that would be all right; she would like the warmth of another body, especially a cuddle with Mum . . .

Weeeek, weeeek . . . a noisy pair of wekas on the beach. She wondered if birds ever got cold too.

Someone was calling her. Sam. Sam. Over and over. And shaking her, none too gently.

'Wake up, Sam. Sam.'

'I can't. Leave me alone.'

'You must, Sam. Wake up.'

'No.'

'Sam, you've got to. Sam, you've got to go now.'

'Go where?'

'Over to Mansion House. To get help.'

She was still dreaming, of course.

'I mean it, Sam. We've got to get help.'

'You said when it's light.'

'No, now. We can't wait until then.'

'Why?'

'Sam, wake up. *Wake up*, I tell you.'

She managed to prise her chin off her knees and open her eyes to the extent of seeing a blurred Tiri light sweep around the horizon far to the south.

'Sam, I'm worried about Dad.' Sam felt one hand on her shoulder, the other pushing back the hair from her cold forehead almost as though trying to lift away the mask of sleep. 'I want you and Jane to leave now, as soon as we've got the dinghy down.'

She wasn't dreaming.

Sam choked on a yawn. 'You're joking.'

'I'm not, Sam. This is for real. When he got back on his bunk he was sick again.'

Sam's eyelids gave up the struggle to stay open.

'Poor Mum.'

'I managed to catch most of it in a towel.'

'Poor Mum . . .' The hand on her shoulder must have known she was dropping off again, because it began to shake her roughly.

'Sam, you must wake up.' Sam's head jerked back with the realization that she was not to be allowed to sleep.

'How long have I been asleep?'

'Only about ten, fifteen minutes.'

'No wonder I feel so ghastly.'

'I know, Sam, I'm sorry, but Dad seems to have become unconscious again, except that he's twitching a lot and his pulse is racing. I don't like it.'

Sam uncurled her arms from around her legs. There was a dull ache behind her eyes and as she turned and looked deeply into the black hills behind the beach, a chill ran down her spine and up again.

'No, Mum. Please. I don't want to go up there in the dark.'

You and Jane will be together. You'll have a torch each, and it will be daybreak soon. It starts to get light around half past five.'

'What's the time now?'

'About three-thirty.'

'That's two hours.'

'It won't be by the time we've got the dinghy down and I've woken Jeremy to look after Dad while I row you ashore. Come on, Sam. Jane's getting some food together.'

Sam could not help gazing at the shadowy beach and the bush through which Mum wanted her to walk. There was something sinister about that beach, she knew. She played her last card.

'If you're so worried, Mum, why can't we send up a flare?'

'I thought of that, Sam, truly I did. But who would see it? Tucked right in here, who would see it? The lighthouse keeper? He doesn't keep watch at four in the morning for any flare which might happen to go off.'

'Someone would.'

'Someone might. Some fishing boat. Then what? We might sit here for hours, worrying about Dad, wondering if someone had seen it, and if so, what they proposed to do about it. Waiting for someone to find us.

Sam, we can't do that. We've got to do something ourselves.'

Sam staggered against the tiller as she stood unsteadily upright, turning her back on the beach.

'Good girl.' A final squeeze from the hand around her shoulder, then she was on her own. She was trying, oh, how she was trying, not to think about that hill behind her. 'Now, let's tackle the dinghy.'

As Sam predicted earlier, it was a formidable challenge. With Sam and Jane taking the weight of the stern and their mother the bow, they inched the cumbersome dinghy towards the liferails. Sam was too tired to make any suggestions at all; dully she followed her mother's curt orders as if in a dream, and Jane was similarly uncommunicative. It seemed impossible to get a comfortable position from which to exert such strength as she had left; shrouds, boom, liferails, spinnaker boom and cabin top left little room for manoeuvre.

Then came the hardest bit: turning the dinghy over until the stern was balanced across the liferails, right-way-up. Now, thought Sam, her chest aching with the effort, it was just a question of lowering it gently, stern first, into the water. But the dinghy went down too fast, its stern dipping deeply into the water and its bow slamming against *Aratika*'s topsides. Sam cringed. Dad's paintwork! As the splash subsided, there was a horrified cry from her mother.

'The painter! Who's got the painter?'

Sam blinked. 'I thought . . .'

'Jane, your torch, quick, in the bow.'

The sharp beam of light showed the dinghy bobbing gently alongside, with several centimetres of water in the bottom, the yellow plastic detergent bottle which served as a bailer floating against its lashing – and the painter curled in a heap in the bow. Mrs Starr thrust her arm

163

down through the liferails, but the dinghy was just out of reach and already drifting away from them.

Mrs Starr scrambled to her feet. Sam felt her push roughly past towards the cockpit, while Jane's torch swung crazily around the deck in a vain attempt to provide light.

'What's she doing?'

'I don't know . . . the dinghy . . .' Sam was too stunned to speak. Their dinghy, their only means of seeking help, was floating off into the dark, half-full of water . . .

A few seconds later, her mother could be heard climbing back along the deck, banging something against the cabin top. Then Jane's torch revealed her with the boathook, leaning outwards from the shrouds, stretched to the very limit of her fingertips and toes. Still the dinghy was out of reach.

The boathook clattered onto the deck while Sam and Jane stared helplessly at the dinghy. There didn't seem to be much they could do about it . . . Sam became aware of the rustle of oilskin and the sound of someone undressing.

'Mum, what . . . ?'

'Isn't it obvious?' she snapped. In the torch beam, they saw she was down to only a pair of pants. 'Keep your torch on the dinghy, Jane.' And before Sam or Jane could say anything she had stepped briskly over the liferails and steadied herself momentarily against the shrouds. Then she was gone, her neat dive making a small tidy splash. Jane's torch searched for a head breaking the surface.

'Keep it on the dinghy,' cried Sam. 'Like she said.'

As the beam of light landed on the dinghy again, they heard the sound of their mother's gasp for air as she surfaced; just like the seals at the zoo, thought Sam, watching her mother, her brave mother, breaststroke the short distance to the dinghy. She could almost feel the cold water wrapping itself around her own body. A shiny arm went up to grab the bow; a hand searched for the painter; and then, spluttering, her mother began to tow the dinghy back to *Aratika*, with the rope clenched between her teeth.

'Good old Mum,' breathed Sam.

'If you'd had the painter, she wouldn't have had to do that,' said Jane spitefully.

'I could say the same about you,' said Sam. 'Don't shine that thing in her face,' she added quickly, seeing her mother wince as the beam shone straight into her eyes, which were wide with fear. Of course: Mum who would never swim off *Aratika* in deep water, Mum who admitted being afraid of the sharks and stingrays and barracouta and all the other big fish they knew were around the gulf. No wonder she looked petrified.

Painfully slowly, the bobbing head drew closer and then Mrs Starr was near enough to reach up with the painter. 'Here, tie a bowline,' she gasped to Sam, and swam away towards the dinghy. Sam could appreciate the effort it took her mother to haul herself over the stern of the dinghy. She pulled on the painter and the dinghy bumped alongside with its huddled and breathless passenger.

It had all taken only a few minutes, yet Sam knew, as she helped her mother climb back on board, that again the tables had turned. It was her turn to be strong. Once more she gently dried her mother's back and arms, retrieved her clothes from the top of the cabin, and chivvied her to get dressed. But this time there was no brandy to help still the chattering of her teeth. Sam directed Jane to start bailing out the dinghy, and went below to find a blanket to wrap around her mother's legs and a dry towel for her hair. In the darkness of the cabin, her father's rasping restless breathing reminded her of the task ahead, but it was her mother who needed what comfort she had to offer. She

165

found another packet of biscuits, and once again they sat together in the cockpit. Several minutes passed. The only sound was the rhythmic splash of water as Jane bailed out the dinghy alongside.

'I'm sorry, Sam,' said Mrs Starr eventually.

'What for? Giving me a fright, you mean?'

'Not that.'

'What then?'

'For calling you three useless kids.'

'Oh, that.' Sam had forgotten. 'So you did.'

'It wasn't fair. Or true.'

Sam was silent, but she gave her mother's shoulder an extra squeeze.

'Dinghy's nearly empty.' Jane's voice cut through their moment of closeness. 'Enough to go ashore, anyway.'

Sam's heart sank as the reality of the situation returned. Ashore meant climbing up a hill, a dark hill of bush and trees and wekas and perhaps other things she dared not name.

'Mum, do we really have to go now?' she said quietly.

'Yes, if you're ready. I know this is a lot to ask of you, Sam.'

Sam was about to say no, she wasn't ready, she was so tired she could barely stand up, when she remembered her father's clammy head, his strange breathing, and Drunks Bay.

'Well? Do you feel up to it?'

'No, I don't. I don't want to, one little bit. But I'll go.'

CHAPTER 18

Over the top

It was all quite unreal, thought Sam, huddled in the stern of the dinghy. Behind them on *Aratika* was the still unconscious, ever restless Dad and a bewildered Jeremy woken from his sleep to be watchkeeper. She shivered with apprehension as the dark arms of the bay slowly came together behind her. She was being drawn into a black hole.

In her lap was a small backpack containing torches, some chocolate, Band-aids in case they got blisters, two apples and a rough sketch of the track they were to follow, taken from Dad's nautical chart of Kawau Island to Rakino Passage. They had found that the track up from the beach was not marked, yet Mrs Starr said she could distinctly remember a good wide track from their walk there last summer; it joined up with the Grey Road along the ridge.

'It's quite steep, then you get to a sort of clearing at the top where there's the remains of a cattle yard or something. The road goes off to the left and you just follow it down to Mansion House. Once you're on the Grey Road there'll be no problems.' She sounded nervous. They were taking a risk leaving Dad in Jeremy's care, but her mother had been adamant that she must keep the dinghy in case she needed to move the anchor.

'You'll find there are signs marking the way to Mansion House. It should take about an hour, maybe less. If you get lost, retrace your steps or wait until daybreak. It won't be long. But you won't get lost. The road is wide enough for a Land Rover. And when you get to Mansion House, tell the first person you see that you need a doctor and help. Get a big yacht to motor around, or a fizz boat.'

'Mum, stop talking,' interrupted Jane.

'Try to get a big boat, with a radio. They can put out a call for a doctor. There'll be someone ashore at Mansion House, even at six in the morning, I'm sure. If not, jump up and down and shout.'

'Mum, stop it,' said Sam sharply.

'Stop what?'

'Stop fussing.'

'I'm not fussing. I'm just . . .'

'You are. We'll be all right,' said Sam. 'We've been over all that.'

'Yes but . . .'

'Mum, we'll be okay,' cried Sam. She could almost hear her mother grinding her teeth.

'Over to the right a bit, Mum,' said Jane, flashing her torch around the rocky shoreline. 'There are some big rocks up the left side of the beach, then it looks clear and sandy.'

Mrs Starr, her breath coming fast and harsh, stopped rowing. 'Shine your torch on the beach, Jane,' she panted. 'Hold it *still*. Okay, I see.' She lined up the dinghy and the oars splashed again.

'We're nearly there,' said Jane suddenly, sounding surprised. Her torch had picked up white waves rolling over the wet sand. Mrs Starr stopped rowing.

'Could you walk from here, Jane?'

'Yes, I think so.'

'Try then.'

They were closer in than they thought; just as Jane clambered out of the dinghy, the bow ran aground on the sandy shallows and a wave, though small, broke into the stern. My wet shorts, made wetter, thought Sam furiously. 'Idiot.'

'Sor-ree,' said Jane, unsympathetic.

168

'How would . . .?'

'Sam, get out,' interrupted Mrs Starr. 'There's no time for that. Got your bag? Torch? Chart?'

Climbing stiffly over the stern, Sam felt the warm water around her ankles as she held the dinghy while her mother shipped the oars and climbed out to turn it around. Her bare feet sank into the soft sand. This was the moment she had been dreading.

'Yes, I've got them.' She watched Jane's torch flashing up and down the beach and into the gully behind. There was flax, some cabbage trees, and some big trees and pungas. She was reluctant to start walking across the wet sand towards the whispering bush; reluctant even to release her grip on the dinghy which rocked as her mother climbed aboard. On an impulse she reached over and her fingers landed on a smooth rounded surface which she recognized as a knee. A hand came down over hers, as cold and as tense, pressing firmly in a gesture of sympathy and farewell.

'Mum,' she said quietly. 'What do we do if we get really lost? Really really lost?

'You won't, Sam. You've got the chart. Look after each other. Now go, Sam.' The hand gave a final strong squeeze. 'Give me a push, will you?'

Sam grasped the stern with both hands and walked a few steps into deeper water before she gave a final shove to the departing dinghy. There was no looking back now.

'Bye, Mum.' Her eyes filled with tears.

'Bye, Sam.'

'Bye, Mum.' Behind her, Jane's voice made her jump.

'Bye, Jane. You'll be back in a couple of hours. Now go, both of you. Please. Go quickly . . .' The sounds of the oars echoed once again around the bay – creak, splash, creak, splash – and then they too were gone.

'Come on, Sam. What are you doing?' Jane sounded impatient.

'I'm coming.' She turned away slowly, taking a last look at the black mast in the bay, and began to walk across the beach towards the searching flash of Jane's torch. Her toes scraped painfully across shells sticking up out of the sand and she found it difficult to keep her balance, staggering a little like a drunken sailor. She noted with some surprise – for there was no moon now, not even a hint – that she could distinguish between the wet sand below and the dry sand above the high-water mark, and even tell where the sand gave way to a grassy bank. Under her feet the dry sand was still slightly warm from the previous day's sun. This was as good a place as any to put on her sandshoes.

'What are you *doing*?' said Jane nearby.

'Getting my sandshoes on. You'll need yours, too. Here.' She tossed them towards the voice. Her fingers groped around inside the pack. 'Here's the map.'

'We won't need it yet. The first bit of track wasn't on the big chart, remember.'

'But Mum did draw it in,' said Sam, tying up her shoelaces. This was what it would be like to be blind. 'She said the track went up the side of a small valley with a stream in it.'

'Hope she's right.'

Sam took a deep breath. Soon she was walking on bristly grass, joining Jane in threading a way between the clumps of flax. Each step was softer and boggier underfoot.

'Over to the left a bit,' said Jane. 'It's awfully wet over here and . . .' Sam heard two sounds together: Jane's sharp intake of breath and a sudden swishing, very close by.

'What's that? Jane!' But Jane's torch had already spotted the cause half-way up a cabbage tree and peering fixedly at the beam.

'An opossum, Sam. Look, an opossum,' she laughed,

relieved, while Sam let out her breath and stared at the culprit. She had forgotten about opossums and suchlike.

'I can see,' she said coldly. 'And what else will we find on this island to scare the daylights out of us?'

The sarcasm was lost on Jane. 'Well, there's thousands of wallabies, of course, and wekas – we've heard plenty of those about, and I think there are rats and bush mice, and I'm not sure about wild pig – and one of the books we've got on Kawau says there might be wild deer but no one has seen any for years . . .'

'Shut up, Jane. I didn't ask for a lecture.'

'But you asked.'

'Okay, I asked. Come on, we shouldn't be looking at opossums.'

'Lead on.'

Sam still found the general atmosphere disturbing. What lay ahead? The torches picked out a large flat area, about the size of a tennis court, underneath a stand of tall creaking trees. At the far end it began to slope upwards, narrowing into a rocky gully: presumably that was where their track followed the stream up the hill.

'Do you think that's the path?' asked Sam doubtfully. She had no recollection at all of walking up through that untidy jumble of rocks.

'I suppose so,' said Jane, swinging her torch to right and left. 'I can't see where else it would go.' Some of her perkiness had gone. She wasn't, noted Sam sourly, quite so eager to take the lead now. There were many times when Sam wished she wasn't the eldest, always having to go first, and never had this feeling been so strong. Jane, the little beast, was waiting for her.

'We'd better go,' she said. They walked quickly across the flat ground and began to search for the track which Mum said went up the gully. Sam's footsteps slowed.

'I can't see a track,' she mumbled. 'Can you?'

'Nope.'

'Mum said it was a good clear track.' Sam was suddenly angry. She was having to pick her way carefully over rocks, around ridges and ledges formed by tangled roots and fallen trees, as the bush closed around her.

'This is silly,' said Sam, coming to a complete stop in front of a high overhang of roots around which she could see no way at all. 'This isn't a track. We *can't* be lost already.'

'Well, there's Mum's stream,' said Jane helpfully, shining her torch over to their left on a pool about half as big as their bath at home. Over it trickled a tiny waterfall.

'Some stream,' snorted Sam. Hands on hips and panting, she straightened up and shone her light on the soft green umbrellas of the pungas above, so thick they formed a complete roof over the stream bed. 'It's all jungly, Jane. I don't like it.'

'Turn your torch off, Sam,' said Jane abruptly.

'What for?'

'Turn it off. You'll see.'

And as her eyes adjusted to a darkness blacker than any she had experienced that night, Sam did see. She was being watched: hundreds of little green eyes were staring at her. She screamed, shutting her eyes to close out the nightmare. If these were opossums, there were enough to constitute an army, a fearsome army of teeth and claws. Why wasn't Jane screaming too? When she opened her eyes, Jane's torch was on and in its wide beam she could see no furry animals, nothing except rocks and tree trunks and the steep slopes of the valley disappearing into oblivion. The torch flicked off – and again the green eyes were looking at her.

'Jane, for God's sake,' she shouted, bursting into tears.

'They're glow-worms, ding-aling,' cried Jane triumphantly. 'Hundreds and hundreds of glow-worms. Look,' she insisted, shining her torch into the overhang formed by twisted roots. Through wet eyes, Sam could see a tiny transparent worm hanging from a thread, then others nearby. Jane flicked off the torch again, and instantly the pale emerald glow appeared, a tiny web of coloured lights. 'Aren't they pretty?'

Sam could only sob. 'Jane . . . we're supposed to be getting help for Dad and we've only been gone ten minutes and we're lost already, and you give me horrible frights, it's not fair . . .'

'Well, this obviously isn't the track, so I suggest we get back to the beach and start again,' said Jane, unrepentant. 'Come on, Sam, you didn't really get a fright.'

'I did.'

'Whoever heard of being frightened by a glow-worm?'

'You can be frightened by anything if you don't know what it is. And I've never heard of glow-worms on Kawau.'

'Perhaps we've discovered them,' said Jane as she started back towards the beach. 'Starr's glow-worm. Well, there can't be many people who've tried to get up this silly valley at night. Up what is obviously *not* the track. The lost glow-worms of Kawau . . .'

'They can't be lost if no one knew they were here in the first place,' said Sam stumbling along behind.

In a surprisingly short time, they could hear the sea and once more found themselves on the flat area under the trees.

'We must have lost at least twenty minutes,' said Sam wearily. 'What's the time?'

'I left my watch on the boat.'

The boat – there she lay, framed by the trees, a tiny pin-prick of light and an uncomfortable reminder that they had a job to do. Up in the bush a morepork hooted.

'You look that way, I'll go this,' said Sam. 'We'd better make sure this time. Mum *said* it was a good clear track.' She moved off in the hope that if she kept repeating this often enough it would turn out to be true. Perhaps they

173

should go right back to the beach and start again, but for some reason she didn't want to leave the shelter of the trees. She paused at the edge of the grass. There was something about this place which had worried her ever since Mum had first announced they were seeking shelter there; something to do with that walk last summer. Then, as her torch lit upon a piece of driftwood so smooth and white she thought it was a bone, she knew what it was: Bosanquet Bay was supposed to be a place of revenge, of battles and cannibal feasts. Dad's voice, best school-teacher style, came back to her, 'Right here, in this grove, so they say, they killed them and ate the lot . . .' They had found a bone too, and although Dad said it was probably that of a cow or sheep from the days when they tried to farm the southern part of the island, Jeremy had kept it just the same.

The canoes would have landed in Bosanquet right in front of her. They would have fought and killed right where she was standing, and from the trees behind gathered wood for their fires. . . This was the 'banqueting hall' Dad had talked about . . .

They had to find the track. There was no other way out of Bosanquet Bay. Wildly, she swung her torch around. The stillness of the bay mocked her; it was the quiet of death.

'Jane, I . . .' But an excited cry interrupted her.

'Here it is, Sam. I think I've found it.' Trembling with fright, Sam turned to look where Jane's spotlight was pointing along a wide track, leading up the side of the valley.

'Let's go,' Sam took off over stones and clumps of dry grass up onto the track. Their torchlights melted together as they set off, Sam leading.

'What's the hurry?'

But Sam couldn't speak. She was panting with terror. The track quickly became very steep and so deeply rutted

174

that she was forced to slow down. She was glad that after fifty metres or so Jane began to wheeze audibly, so that neither of them was capable of talking much.

'Wait on, Sam.'

'No.'

'You're still going too fast.'

'Doubt it.'

'You *are*.'

But Sam was slowing down; not because of Jane's protests but because her legs refused to respond to her will. She dared not stop or look behind, even once.

'Gosh, Sam,' grumbled Jane. 'What's got into you?'

'Nothing . . . tell you later . . . come *on*.'

'No, I'm puffed out.' She had stopped, Sam realized, as the torch beam clicked off and the sound of sandshoes on loose stones ceased. Sam was forced to stop too, and look back down the track. Jane was bending with stitch.

'Come on, Jane, *please*.'

'What's the sudden hurry?'

'Dad's the hurry, isn't he? Come on, we've only just started.' Guiltily – for wasn't it a bit mean to use Dad as an excuse? – she turned and shone her torch upwards. The track rose steeper than ever. On the left side towered closely growing manuka, their tall skinny trunks grinding and creaking together. Down below on the right must be the glow-worm valley; so the track, thought Sam, didn't run up the side of the stream as Mum had said.

Jane's voice echoed her thoughts.

'Mum said,' she panted, 'that when we get up over this hill, it's downhill all the way.'

'I don't believe her.' Or any adult ever again, she resolved silently. Dad and his fine weather. Mum and her silly track. From the beach a weka called, to be answered by others from the far side of the valley. 'Wee*eeek*, wee*eeek*.' She wondered if the screams of battle had rung as clear and harsh around the bay. 'Morepork . . . morepork,' cried the little owl.

Her legs were aching and she could scarcely breathe, but she slogged upwards, hardly caring whether Jane was keeping up with her or not. The track, she reasoned, had to reach the top of the ridge sometime. All her attention was focussed on the few metres ahead.

Through the pounding in her ears she heard a cry.

'Look, Sam!' She raised her eyes to follow the line of the track. At the top was a small square of pearly sky, clearly the crest of the ridge.

'That . . . *must* be . . . the top?' gasped Jane.

'Yes.' Sam gave a gulp of relief. Every time they looked towards that square of sky if seemed as far away as ever until, just as Sam's legs had reached a point of pain she had never experienced before, the bush fell away from either side and she stumbled out onto a wide grassy plateau swept by a fresh wind.

There were the cattle pens, just as Mum had said. To the left her shaking torch picked up the wheelmarks on the Grey Road winding down the ridge. There was the rest of Kawau stretching darkly in front of her to the north. To the west were the lights of the mainland and the lights signposting the sea in between. Her hot eyes followed the line of the coast to the south, to the city far away and the faithful Tiri lighthouse.

And further, to the east? Between Tiri Island and the black mass of Kawau's highest hills ran a strip of distant sea, glowing with the first hint of daybreak.

Jane came up gasping alongside her and flopped down on the grass.

'Why didn't you . . . my legs . . .'

But Sam could only gaze at the lightening horizon, her eyes wet with tears. Even through her pain she felt its promise of renewed hope.

'Jane, look', she breathed. 'There's the dawn.'

They sat in silence, their backs to the wind. Above them were great clumps of cloud giving no hint of where the moon was hiding.

'Can we see the boat from up here?' said Jane, still gasping for air as she fumbled with the fastenings on Sam's backpack.

Sam had almost forgotten the boat and the three people on board. Perhaps she should thank her mother for not reminding her of Bosanquet's history before saying goodbye on the beach. She would never have agreed to go, had she known.

'I don't think so.' Dark fists of land obscured a clear view down into the bay itself, but if she squinted there was a tiny pinpoint of light just above where the entrance to Bosanquet might be. It was so faint that the next time she blinked, it was gone. If it was *Aratika*, she was certainly anchored well out. What would a light mean – Dad having convulsions, or Mum making a cup of tea?

'Here's your chocolate.' Sam heard the crack as Jane broke the block in half. Her share was the size of a playing card, and Sam ate it all greedily, in one go. It stuck to her teeth, but it was sweet and warm in her mouth.

'Got the chart?' she said.

'Here. But we won't need it,' said Jane. 'There's the track, clear as clear. Couldn't be anything else.'

'Okay, but I still want to look. Shine your torch on here.' She flattened the scruffy bit of paper over a smooth patch of earth. 'We're here . . . and that other road over to South Cove goes off somewhere along this ridge.'

'It looks longer than I thought,' said Jane. 'Mum can't draw, can she?' Where Mansion House was supposed to be she had tried to draw a picture of a house with verandahs and big trees. 'What a mess.'

'I'd like to see you do better, after what she's had to cope with tonight,' said Sam.

'Yes, what did go on while I was asleep?'

'Oh . . . tell you later,' said Sam, folding up the chart and struggling to her feet. The events of the night were still too fresh in her memory for sharing, even with Jane.

'I hate being fobbed off.'

'Later,' Sam said firmly. 'Let's go.'

'I want my apple,' said Jane. 'Stand still.'

Sam felt her pull down on the pack as she reached inside.

'You too?'

'May as well,' Sam said, taking a last look at the pink flush along the horizon while Jane did up the buckles. She hoisted the pack into a more comfortable position on her shoulders. 'Come on. Next stop Mansion House.'

Walking off down the road as she bit into her apple, Sam found it difficult to get a rhythm going. Her legs, grown cold during their rest, had lost all feeling and seemed to be moving entirely of their own accord. At least it was downhill now, and a comparatively even surface. And the darkness was yielding to a drab grey.

Scrubby manuka closed in around the track and the steady downhill slope gave way to a series of roller-coasters which once again had them struggling for breath. This was wallaby country, Sam knew, and it wasn't long before they came around a corner and startled a small group of three or four sitting on the road. Their torches followed them bouncing off along the track and into the undergrowth. Normally the sight of wallabies had Jane jumping up and down with excitement, thought Sam, but she too had settled into a grim plodding silence.

Old tea-trees gave way to old pines and still the road stretched ahead. Sam realized dully that her torch was now hardly necessary, so she switched it off and found that her eyes adjusted easily to the growing daylight. Jane, without speaking, did the same. Colour was coming back into the world: the intense green of ferns at the side of the road, a grove of lilies. Sounds too, as the birds

178

awoke. Sam vaguely registered the throaty call of a tui nearby. She glanced behind at Jane. She was a small figure in a yellow parka, bare legs, sandshoes, with her eyes down and hair sticking out all over, trudging along the track. Sam supposed she looked much the same, but worse. She was conscious of scratches all over her legs and of eyes which felt sunk deep into her head with tiredness.

The road wound through stands of tall pine trees above a carpet of pungas. Along the ridge above the Copper Mine, she saw the sea, glowing turquoise now, and then the brick chimney down on the rocks, pointing upwards like an up-ended pistol. She felt a faint surge of hope. They had sailed past the Copper Mine often enough and she knew that the Mansion House was not far around the point. Yet the road seemed interminable. They passed two or three new signposts to South Cove, Schoohouse Bay, Copper Mine, Lady's Bay; they wanted none of those, only the straight and downhill course of the coach road to Mansion House.

Sam and Jane had not spoken for over an hour of walking. There seemed to be an understanding that they wouldn't stop or talk until they reached Mansion House Bay. Sam's new fear was her own body; not the sea, nor the dark, nor her mother's ability to sail, nor the ghosts of the bush, but her own small body which had had no rest. Several times they stumbled on this final stretch, helping each other silently to their feet, resuming the weary walk without a pause to brush the stones off skinned knees and bruised hands.

All Sam could think about was Mansion House where there would be yachts, people and help. She needed only to think of the bump on Dad's forehead and his confused speech, or of Mum's slight body shivering violently in the torchlight after her swim . . . and her exhausted legs responded for a few more metres and another bend in the road.

There seemed to be grass ahead, down at the end of that stretch, around a sharp bend. Smooth green grass like their lawn at home. It *was* a lawn and on it a peacock was strutting.

'Jane, we're there!' Her voice had found a new strength and her legs also, enough to break into an untidy sort of run. The road opened out in front of them into a park-like valley. Now they were both running: past all sorts of strange trees, several more peacocks, some large wekas picking over an upturned rubbish basket, past several small buildings on the right, through a trellis archway towards Mansion House standing pale grey and square to the left of the road and facing the sea. They ran on: past a white picket fence, the imposing front porch and the graceful arch of the verandahs, and on towards the wharf.

But not quite onto the wharf. Sam, leading, found herself skidding to a halt, her arms flailing about and her backpack falling off her shoulders. She stared aghast at the empty water. Where they had expected to find a bay full of yachts, there was not a single boat in sight.

CHAPTER 19

Mansion House

Sam stood and licked her dry lips. Behind her the sound of Jane's footsteps on the concrete also stopped abruptly. They stood together, hand in hand, gasping for breath, unbelieving.

This was not the peaceful bay they had expected, the sheltered haven where *Aratika* had so often dropped anchor. A wind was stinging their hot cheeks and driving choppy waves up the beach; it was a northerly, the same northerly of the night before, and that was why there were no boats in the bay.

'There . . . there they all are,' said Jane, pointing. Over on the other side of the harbour, tucked into small bays along the northern arms of Bon Accord, sheltered from the wind, lay the race fleet. Half a kilometre away, at least. Too far to be of any help.

Holding hands, they walked slowly out to the end of the wharf, still hardly believing what the wind and their eyes were telling them, hoping that a yacht, just one yacht, would appear, perhaps around the point in Two-House Bay. But Sam knew only too well that no skipper worth his salt would lie anywhere near Mansion House in a northerly.

She sat down on the steps at the end of the wharf, totally drained of energy, thought, ideas, of all emotion except anger.

'Mum forgot. She bloody well forgot. Why didn't she think? To send us all this way for nothing! Why didn't she remember the wind?' Tears of frustration welled up until she was crying uncontrollably.

'Sam, that's history,' said Jane sullenly. 'We're here. Mum's over there.'

'All this way – for nothing,' repeated Sam, standing up. Driven by anger, she stomped back along the wharf. There was a light on upstairs, but otherwise Mansion House lay silent.

'There must be something . . . someone . . .'

'A telephone,' said Jane. Together they peered in through the bay windows, through a hundred years of time into a world of wooden pillars, tapestries, heavy furniture, gold-framed paintings. There was a peculiar square-shaped piano, marble busts and polished floors.

'Telephone? In there?' scorned Sam. She ran along underneath another verandah. 'Nor here either,' she said, as a huge dining-room table set with silver candlesticks and flowery china met her eyes. 'They didn't have telephones in those days, thicko.'

'There must be one somewhere. What about a public phone box, a red one?'

'I've never seen one. Have you?'

Jane didn't rise to the sarcasm. Together they ran further round to the side of the building.

'Here's the kitchen,' said Jane, her nose flat against another window.

'So?' They were at the back of the building now, behind a wall of grey concrete and small windows, all closed. Except one, but its significance was lost on Sam.

They returned to the front porch. Sam, growing more desperate with every second, banged as hard as she dared on the glass of the French doors. From a pedestal inside, a white marble head stared coldly back.

'No use doing that,' said Jane. 'You'll only break the glass. We know there's no one there. No one sleeps in a museum.'

Sam backed away from the porch, defeated. There was a lump in her throat, a sense of failure and of not knowing where to turn.

'Jane, damn you, don't you understand anything?

182

Mum's sitting in that boat around there and for all we know Dad might have had a fit by now, or been sick again, or jumped overboard thinking he was somewhere else. Or died, even.' Her voice was echoing off the wall of the house above her.

'Don't shout at me.'

'Don't you see?'

'Yes, I do see.'

'All you can do is make stupid remarks . . .'

'Doubt it . . .'

'. . . and stand there looking useless . . .'

'I'm tired too, you know,' Jane shot back.

Sam walked away, boiling over with rage and frustration, scratching her face against the overhanging frond of some peculiar sort of palm tree. She had to sit down. The low seawall dividing the sand from the green lawn seemed as good a place as any. She slung her pack furiously onto the ground and flopped down. Through tears, she noticed that Jane had followed and was sitting quietly a little further along. For a few minutes, nothing was said.

'There are all those boats over there,' said Jane eventually.

'So?'

'We could flash a message with a mirror.'

'You got a mirror?'

'We might find one in the sand.'

'Start looking.'

Another silence. Jane tried again.

'What day is it?'

'Don't know.'

'You must know.'

'No more than you.'

Jane thought for a bit. 'Saturday. Yesterday was Friday. Yesterday we had school.'

'Suppose so.' Was it only yesterday?

'On Saturdays in the summer, lots of people visit Mansion House from the mainland.'

'Suppose so. Later on they do. Not for hours yet.'

'How do you know that?'

'Most places – shops and things – don't open until nine or ten o'clock. And have you seen any ferries around?'

'What's the time now?'

'Haven't a clue.'

Quite suddenly the sun appeared on the green mainland hills behind Kawau.

'There's a dinghy over there,' said Jane. 'Look. We can row over to the other side.'

'What with?'

'Oars.'

'Where from?'

'Underneath perhaps.'

'Go and look.' Sam knew it was good seamanship to take your oars home. Jane ran along the beach and peered underneath the upturned dinghy pulled up on the sand. 'Well?'

'Couldn't we paddle with our hands?' She was beginning to sound as desperate as Sam was feeling.

'Against that wind and all that chop? We'd never make it.'

Jane picked up a shell and tried to spin it across the surface of the water, but the wind blew it back. 'I'm so thirsty,' she wailed.

'Me too,' agreed Sam. This they could do something about as there was usually a tap on the end of wharves. 'Over there, come on.' They stumbled along the beach, climbed up onto the wharf and near the end found a tap low down, but not too low to bend and slurp greedily at the water in their cupped hands.

Sam, finishing first, leaned against the white railing and wiped her wet hands across her forehead. In the green water below a school of wriggling sprats swam lazily.

Despite the momentary pleasure of fresh water in her mouth and on her face, a sort of deadly tiredness was creeping over her; that awful craving for sleep seemed to be overcoming her anger and her worry. She must not forget why they were here, on the end of Mansion House wharf at six or seven in the morning, and why *Aratika* was not lying over there snugly with all those other boats. She decided it was no use waving her arms up and down. They would never see her. Her eyes wandered vaguely around the features of the bay. She knew there was nothing around the lefthand point. Around the righthand point was . . . she tried to remember, thinking of the times when *Aratika* sailed in to anchor . . . a house surely, a funny square-looking house. She even thought, as she stared at the point dividing the two bays, that she saw a figure on the rocks far beyond, but after rubbing her eyes, she decided it had been an illusion. That was too much to hope for. A house would be enough.

It was worth trying. It was the only thing left to try.

'Jane,' she began cautiously. 'Do you remember seeing a house around the point?'

Still splashing her face vigorously with water, Jane looked up.

'Where?'

'Behind those rocks. Round in the next bay.'

'Don't remember. What about it?'

'Don't be thick. If there is . . . Turn the tap off, Jane. You're wasting a lot of water.'

'We're not going to walk around there, are we?'

'What else do you suggest?'

'I couldn't walk another step.'

'It's not far. Come on.' She set off along the wharf.

'What if there is a bach but it's all shut up and empty like Mansion House?'

'Then we might be able to break in and find a

185

telephone,' said Sam, her pace increasing slightly as she convinced herself that there was a house.

'Break in? Really?'

'Why not—if someone's sick and needs help.'

'What if there's no one there *and* no telephone either?'

'Gosh, you're a pain. Then,' said Sam firmly, 'we'll have to walk further back, around to Schoolhouse. There are baches there.' She had just remembered the various paths and signposts they had passed on the road down. But more walking, and uphill? She wasn't too sure she had that sort of energy left. At the land end of the wharf she noticed a large brown and green board.

'Hauraki Gulf Maritime Park Board,' she read, but her eyes were too tired to make any sense of the map with its squiggly white lines and arrows and names. She could think only of that square little house in the next bay.

'I'd like to break into a house,' said Jane chattily, catching up as Sam set off across the lawn. 'What do you think we could use? Break a window might be best.'

'You're hopeless,' said Sam, but she couldn't resist a smile.

They had crossed the wide lawn above the seawall and climbed across the thick outspread roots of a great tree at the far end of the beach. Now they could see a steep track leading up from the beach and obviously going around the point. There was a notice there.

'Two-House Bay,' read Jane. 'You're right Sam.' And then she read, ' "Ranger". What's "ranger"?'

Sam stared at the wooden sign, hope springing up.

'A ranger's a man who . . . Come on, Jane. That's him. That must be him I saw!'

'Who? You didn't tell me you'd seen anyone,' shouted Jane after her.

'I thought I was seeing things.'

'Wait for me . . .'

Only a little way up the narrow track, its clay surface

186

slippery with loose stones and pine needles, and again she was fighting against the pain in her legs. She heard Jane cry out, a howl of hurt and anger; perhaps she had fallen over, but Sam could not, dared not, stop. Jane would have to look after herself. She ran on, stumbling over roots and wooden steps set neatly into the slope, trying not to look to the left where the path dropped steeply to the rocks below. The track ran upwards, twisting back on itself, and still she had to keep climbing.

It had to end soon. There was a house in the next bay. There had to be.

Dad was talking to her. Nice place, Drunks. God knows where that northerly has come from . . . I should have seen it earlier . . . sometimes quite a hairy ride to Kawau . . . And, what's the hurry? Are you looking for someone?

Except that it wasn't Dad talking now. Just where the track ran along the crest and started to fall away into the next bay, Sam stopped. Walking towards her was a tall figure in khaki shorts and he was talking, smiling at her, his eyes concerned and kind and crinkly, and he was the answer to everything.

CHAPTER 20

Mission accomplished?

Much later, when they were back at last in Auckland, Sam found that her memories of what happened next – after she met the ranger – were very confused. She remembered standing on the path, bursting into tears, trying to explain what had happened and what they wanted. Jane came staggering up over the crest of the hill to join them, absolutely furious, blood dripping down her leg from a nasty graze.

The ranger was a patient man who listened quietly, squatting on one knee in front of her, his hand on her shoulder. Then he picked Jane up in a great fatherly scoop, took Sam by the hand, and led her slowly down the track. She had been right about the house. There it was, a small white house sitting squarely on a lawn in the middle of the bay.

There was a nice motherly lady inside and several small children running round in their pyjamas. Drinks of orange she remembered, and being wrapped in blankets; and food – scrambled eggs and home-made bread, though strangely neither she nor Jane had been very hungry and the food made them feel slightly sick. And while they ate, the magic sounds of the ranger talking on the radio-telephone in another room, calling the yachts in the bay opposite, calling for a doctor and a boat prepared to motor immediately around to Bosanquet Bay. The adult world had taken charge again. She did remember the voice very clearly; it was surprisingly gentle and quiet for such a rugged-looking man.

They had been offered beds then, soft warm beds with hot-water bottles.

'Or I'm wondering,' said the ranger-man, 'if you would rather go straight back around to Bosanquet with the doctor. You can sleep there.'

They glanced at each other. Sam wondered if she looked as terrible as Jane, her little head poking up out of a thick blanket, all eyes and spiky hair. The temptation was enormous, but Sam knew that she, for one, wanted more than anything else to get back to *Aratika*.

'Of course you do,' said the ranger before either of them could reply. 'Nothing beats your own mum and dad, does it? I think you'll last, you two. You're a couple of little toughies.'

He looked out through the wide porch windows. 'It won't be long. Here they come now.' Around the point came a huge white ketch under power, slicing through the waves.

'We're going to have a ride on that?' said Jane, staring.

'If you want to go with them, yes. It's not quite as fast as my runabout, but a good deal more comfortable in these conditions. From what you've told me, I don't think a few minutes are going to make any difference.'

Sam could only nod. The ranger smiled down at her.

'Mission accomplished, eh?'

Not quite, thought Sam. Only after she knew that nothing awful had happened to Dad while they were away, and that he was going to be all right, would the mission be accomplished.

'Let's go then. Keep your rugs around you.'

The sun was on the hills opposite but not yet on the anchored fleets of yachts, as they all went down to the wharf. Sam held fast to the ranger's rough hand, his strong young wife carried Jane, and their three children scampered around.

Curious faces watched as ropes were thrown and shouts exchanged; sturdy arms helped them climb aboard and guided them down to the main cabin and onto bright blue bunks. Gentle hands covered them with more blankets and adjusted the pillows under their heads and felt their pulses. Sam decided that she liked being made a fuss of.

Then there were shouts of farewell and the echoing of heavy feet along the deck above. The whispering engine clicked into gear and accelerated to a high-pitched purr. A woman sat on the end of her bunk, and someone shouted 'Cheerio, see you later,' and she realized she hadn't thanked the ranger or said goodbye to him. . . Even before the big ketch was around the point, Sam and Jane were drifting off to sleep.

CHAPTER 21

Saturday

There was warm sunlight on Sam's face and she sensed someone was sitting on the side of her bed, watching her. Earlier it had been a woman, but this was no woman, this was . . . Sam launched herself at her father.

'You're not dead,' she whispered.

'Not yet.'

'And you're not acting peculiar?'

'No more than usual.'

'And you're not going to hospital?'

'Yes, I am. Right now. Only for an X-ray,' he added quickly as Sam, alarmed, pulled her head away from his shoulder. 'Just to make sure nothing is amiss. The doc doesn't think there is anything to worry about.'

Sam rested her head on the broad plane of his shoulder, her eyes closing, satisfied. Through her half-conscious mind, she noticed a faint smell of soap, a dry T-shirt beneath her cheek. He was going to be all right.

'So you didn't have convulsions or anything?'

'Apparently not. I just woke about seven o'clock feeling like death warmed up and found the boat anchored rather a long way out in Bosanquet Bay. It took me a while to work out where we were. The cabin was in one hell of a mess. Your mother was wearing oilies, propped up against the bulkhead trying valiantly not to sleep and failing. You and Jane were nowhere to be found.'

'Poor Dad,' said Sam. 'You must have wondered what on earth was going on.'

'I did. I couldn't remember coming into Bosanquet. I couldn't remember anything much. Then I saw this ruddy great ketch come steaming around the point straight towards us. I woke Mum and she got upset and this beautiful blonde came aboard like something out of a James Bond movie and started ordering me around. And then I started putting two and two together.'

'What beautiful blonde?'

'That one up there.' Up where? Sam opened her eyes again, remembering now that she was on the big ketch. There was Jane, a hump under the blankets on the other bunk, and through the hatchway a small group of people sat in the cockpit drinking coffee. One of them was a woman with shoulder-length blonde hair. 'That one,' said Dad, smiling. 'She's the doctor you went all that way to fetch.'

Sam gaped. She had imagined a brisk old man peering over his glasses like their own family doctor. That was the lady, she remembered now, who had taken charge of them when they first came aboard and felt their pulses and tucked them up.

'What did she do?'

'Gave me a good going over. Peered into my eyes and felt my pulse and asked me all sorts of questions. Not all of which I was able to answer, I must admit. Mum filled in the gaps.'

'What about last night? Do you remember waking up and being sick? Or coming on deck after we'd anchored? You were all mixed up; you gave us an awful fright. Do you remember that?'

'Not really—oh very vaguely, like one of those dreams you can't quite remember. But I don't feel too bad now, considering. The X-ray's just a double check to make sure. The doc wants me to stay in hospital overnight. She says I'll have an impressive black eye for a couple of weeks,' he added.

'We needn't have gone all that way over the hill then?' She was feeling utterly deflated. 'Mum panicked.'

Her father reacted quickly. 'No, Sam, she didn't.' He

was looking at her very straight. 'You did need to get help, make no mistake. For your mother's sake as well as for mine. She had to know it wasn't anything really bad. It could have been, you know. Head injuries must always be taken seriously.'

Sam nodded, satisfied. She gave an enormous yawn and kicked the blankets off the bunk.

'From what Mum has told me,' her father went on, 'you and Jane, but especially you, did a first-class job last night.' He bent over and kissed her on the forehead. 'Thanks. Lots of thanks,' he said simply.

'That's okay.'

'Now, we'd better get you back to the boat. I have to go soon.'

Sam tried to get out of the bunk, but her legs seemed to have seized up. 'What's wrong, Dad?' she cried in dismay. 'My legs . . .'

'You're stiff, that's all,' laughed Dad. 'I'm not surprised. That was a long walk on top of everything else.' Painfully, Sam managed to stand up.

'What's the time?'

'Around eight, I think. You've only been asleep an hour or so. You can go straight back to sleep on *Aratika*.'

'Where's Mum?'

'Over on our boat. I wouldn't be surprised if she was asleep. Jeremy's fishing. He seems to be the only one of us who's had anything like a normal night's sleep. I think he's a bit sore at missing out on all the fun.'

Sam wasn't interested in Jeremy. 'Is Mum all right?' she asked with a sudden intense urge to see her, hug her, share with her this warm, pleasant feeling of a job well done.

'Yes, but very tired. Are you coming?' he added, as Sam dropped down again on the edge of the bunk, her legs still aching from the effort of standing up. 'They'll loosen up as you move around, Sam.'

She looked reluctantly up into the cockpit. She felt like

193

an intruder and too tired to talk, especially to the sort of smart people who owned such magnificence. All this grandeur made her feel uncomfortable. She wanted to get back to the familiarity of *Aratika*, bare and even shabby by comparison, but cosy and her own.

Her father was waiting for her to go first up the companion-way.

'Here she is,' said a loud male voice as she pulled herself out into the sunlight. 'Now we can meet the young lady properly.' There was a round of introductions – 'my elder daughter Sam, second mate of the *Aratika*,' Dad was saying with such gusto that she squirmed inwardly. She remembered none of their names, except that the doctor was called Susan something. Compliments followed, wafting over Sam like a warm mist. She couldn't concentrate on the adult talk, full of references to the sudden and unexpected wind change during the race, and the usual yachties' yarns.

Sam was wondering how Dad was supposed to be getting off to hospital, when she noticed a figure in *Aratika's* cockpit.

'There's Mum,' she said, interrupting. She stood and waved.

'Tell her we're coming,' said her father. Mrs Starr was waving back. 'I'm surprised she's awake.'

'She did you proud last night,' said the bearded man whom Sam took to be the skipper. 'In my experience, these boating women know more than they think they do. The ones who put their minds to it. The other sort, the ones who go along for the ride, kids and all, shouldn't be allowed.'

The doctor, giving Sam the slightest suggestion of a wink, stood up.

'I think,' she said pleasantly, 'I'd like to see my patient on his way now.' She turned to Sam. 'I want your father to go to Auckland Hospital for an X-ray and twenty-four

194

hours under observation. We're taking him to Sandspit. I'm reasonably happy, but he was unconscious for quite a while and an X-ray is standard practice after a knock like that. You and your mother were absolutely right to seek help the quickest way you could.'

Sam blushed under the doctor's direct gaze. She sought her father's hand.

'There's no need for a helicopter or amphibian – anyway, it's not good for people with head injuries to go in aeroplanes. I've already arranged for an ambulance to meet us at Sandspit at ten,' the doctor continued. 'We'll leave as soon as you and your sister are back on board your own boat with your mother, and you have completed your arrangements, Mr Starr.'

'I wish I could come with you,' Sam said to her father.

'Fancy a ride in an ambulance, do you?'

'No, not that. To keep you company.' She hated the idea of him being put into an ambulance and carted off to hospital by complete strangers.

'Thanks Sam, but I'll be fine. Mum needs you more than I do – to sail the boat home, for one thing.'

The very thought made her tired. She'd had enough sailing to last a lifetime.

'Chin up, Sam,' said her father, gently squeezing the hand he still held. 'Don't look so miserable. You can take it easy today and have a nice relaxed trip home tomorrow. I'll meet you at home tomorrow night.'

'The forecast is good,' said the doctor. 'If this northerly holds, a run all the way. Although it might go round to the west. Even better.' She was speaking to Sam, sailor to sailor. Sam liked that.

'No spinnakers,' said Sam firmly. As acting first mate, she'd earned that.

'No spinnakers,' agreed the doctor gravely.

'What, not even the little . . .'

'Dad,' warned Sam. He grinned.

'Mum's waiting.' Sam looked over again at *Aratika*. Her mother was standing on the cabin top, trying to do something about the bulges in the mainsail. 'We're coming,' called Dad. She looked up and waved. That's some tough lady, my mother, thought Sam as she climbed stiffly down into the dinghy, took the oars, and smiled farewell to the two figures leaning over the ketch's shining rail.

'We'll be back in a few minutes to pick up Jane,' Mr Starr said pushing the dinghy clear of the ketch.

The water shone like polished greenstone. As she swung the oars into a slow rhythm, Sam felt a strong sense of coming home. She stroked gently, glad that her father had allowed her the pleasure of rowing him for a change.

'Here's Dad and Sam,' she heard her mother call. Mum's hair was combed, she had on a fresh T-shirt and she was smiling as the dinghy came alongside. Sam took the painter, climbed over the liferail and busied herself tying a bowline around the stanchion. For some unaccountable reason, she was feeling shy – of her own mother! Then she looked down at the person in the cockpit. Her mother's whole face was a smile of pride and she was holding out her hand.

'Come here, Sam.' She patted the seat alongside and when Sam sat down, she put her arm around her shoulder. Sam felt something snap inside her and she buried her head against her mother's breast.

'I love you, Mum.' She wasn't crying exactly, but her eyes were hot and wet and there was a warm feeling in her chest so intense that she thought she might explode.

'I love you too, Sam.' Both arms were around her. 'You'll be needing a good long sleep now.'

Sam nodded. She wished this moment would last for ever. Then she said, 'You didn't tell me about Bosanquet.'

'What about it?' Was she teasing or had she forgotten? Sam couldn't tell.

'The cannibal feasts and that.'

'Oh, that.' One hand was stroking her forehead, smoothing back hair bristly with salt water, just as she had done in the dark. 'Well, if I had . . .'

'I mightn't have gone.'

'Quite likely. But does this bay look sinister to you now?' she asked innocently, waving an arm at the peaceful scene. 'All that was hundreds of years ago.'

'Not hundreds.'

'Well, one hundred. Anyway, you're glad I didn't, surely? Was it very awful?'

Sam disengaged herself and sat back. Some things were too deep to tell even her mother. 'I'm stiff,' she said.

Mrs Starr nodded. 'And how did you get help in the end? I heard some garbled story from the doctor about your meeting the ranger on the path.'

'We were going over to Two-House Bay to find him.' She had almost forgotten the other bone she had to pick with her mother, that awful anticlimax of finding the bay empty.

'Why? Couldn't you raise anyone on a boat?'

Sam looked carefully at her father, now sitting on the other side of the cockpit.

'Were they all asleep?' Mrs Starr went on. 'Worn out after the race, I suppose. Or hung-over, more likely.'

'There weren't any. Boats in the bay, I mean,' said Sam finally.

'Ha,' cried her father. 'Of course not! In a northerly?'

Sam stole another look at her mother. She seemed so embarrassed that Sam felt really sorry for her. 'You had lots to think about. You couldn't think about everything, Mum,' she said. 'I'll forgive you.' Her mother was clearly having trouble looking Dad in the eye.

'Not to worry, Mum,' he smiled, putting his big hand on her knee in a matey gesture. 'No skipper is infallible.'

'I'll remember that,' she said promptly.

197

'She was a pretty good skipper last night,' said Sam stoutly, anxious to make up lost ground. 'You should have seen her dragging you along the deck. And getting the spinnaker down when the wind changed. And the spinnaker pole. And she was seasick twice and fainted and . . .'

'Not now, Sam,' her mother interrupted, but her voice was gentle.

'You fainted . . .!' said Mr Starr.

'Twice, she did,' said Sam proudly. 'And then she had to go for a swin in the spooky dark because the dinghy floated away and . . .'

'Sam, please. Later,' said Mrs Starr. But Sam was gratified to see a new look of respect in her father's eye as he stared at them both.

'I see you've got quite a story to tell, Louise,' he said quietly. Sam looked away. In family talk, Mum was Mum. Louise was kept for adults and, she thought, when her parents were alone.

'One thing I will say, though,' said her mother. 'Sam did her bit, and more. When I ran out of steam, it was Sam who kept me going. She's a good helmsman, especially sailing to windward. We didn't know that, did we?'

'No indeed. If you can sail a boat to windward at night, Sam, doing it all by feel, you can sail anything.'

Sam thought back over those long hours when she and her mother had shared the helming. Apart from the misery of cold and fear, what did she remember? The splintered flash of the Tiri light, the rising moon's path, the sharp black silhouette of her mother's figure against the sky, the pale grey of the great mainsail.

'Night time's not really all that dark – I mean really black dark,' she said finally. 'It's more lots of greys. You can see quite a lot, really.'

'You're right, Sam,' said Mrs Starr. 'It was my first night sail, too – I had the same impression.'

There was a brief silence. Sam yawned. 'You know, Mum, I think you know more about sailing than you let on.'

'No, I . . .'

'Honestly now, Mum?' her father interjected. 'When you had to take charge, wasn't it easier than you imagined?'

'Easier? A boat like this? You're joking.'

'But you did, didn't you?' persisted Dad. 'You could have sent up a flare but instead you sorted yourselves out, coped with me, sailed on, made a sound decision to run for shelter. You anchored the boat safely and got the sails down. What more do you want?'

Mrs Starr was grinning now. 'Go and do a boatmaster course. Learn a bit about navigation. Stand up to . . .'

'Caught a fish,' yelled Jeremy from the bowsprit, nearly overbalancing in his excitement. 'Dad, a fish,' he screamed, pulling from the sea a wriggling sprat or small schnapper all of fifteen centimetres long. They laughed.

'Coming, Jeremy,' called his father, adding casually as he made his way for'ard, 'You didn't think of knocking up the caretaker at Mansion House, Sam?'

'What caretaker?'

'There's a caretaker there somewhere. Lives in a flat at the back, I think.'

Of course, the open window and the light. It was Sam's turn to look bashful, but happily for her a shout from the ketch provided a diversion.

'That's Jane,' said Sam. 'They're bringing her over. They seem to be making a bit of a fuss.'

Her mother was looking agitated. 'She was all right when the ketch picked you up, wasn't she?'

'I don't remember that bit too well, Mum. But she seemed okay.'

Dad had climbed back into the cockpit, leaving Jeremy swinging a newly-baited line into the water. All three silently watched the approaching grey rubber dinghy powered by a small outboard. Sam could see now that Jane was pale and seemed to have been crying.

The dinghy bounced alongside *Aratika* and Jane was helped aboard and down onto the cockpit seat. White and bewildered, she stared at her father.

He was smiling gently. 'Welcome back . . .' he began, but Jane's immediate response was to burst into tears.

'Sam tells me it was a long hard slog over the hill,' he said, putting his arms round her. For once in her life, Jane had nothing to say. Sam, feeling a new tenderness for her sister, moved across the cockpit to cuddle her close. Jane wasn't such a tough-guy after all.

Mr Starr disengaged himself from the family cuddle. 'I've got to be going.' He kissed the tops of their heads in turn, Mum last. 'Well done, my girls. Now you can all go and get some sleep.'

'Bye, Nick. Take care.'

'Bye, Dad.'

'Hooray, Dad,' called Jeremy.

Mr Starr changed places in the dinghy with the man who was to help sail *Aratika* around to Mansion House and the dinghy zoomed its way across to the waiting ketch. They heard the rattle of the anchor chain and the soft purr of the engine. Within two minutes the big yacht had slipped out around the point.

'I should have gone with him,' said Mrs Starr sadly after a long silence. 'That was a big act, all that hearty stuff. You don't get rid of a splitting headache that easily.'

She sighed heavily, while Jane sniffed into her blanket. 'Come on, you two. Sleep now. Dad's in good hands.'

'What about you, Mum? When are you going to sleep?'

'Later. Jim and I will engine around to Mansion House. I'll sleep then.' Sam had momentarily forgotten the presence of the crew from the ketch who had tactfully seated himself by the mast.

'I'll sleep then, too,' said Sam.

Ten minutes later, with Jane settled on a bunk below, they weighed anchor. Sam was not sorry to leave Bosanquet Bay, for all its present beauty; she would not easily forget those dark moments on the beach.

'Wind's gone around to the west,' said Mrs Starr from the helm as they chugged around the south-west point of Kawau and set a northerly course to Bon Accord Harbour past the Beehive and the Copper Mine and the sharp point of Martello Rock, its long submarine shape hidden by the tide.

They had joined a long line of yachts, most of them under spinnaker, returning to Bon Accord Harbour for the finish of the Saturday race around Kawau Bay. As Mansion House came into sight, her mother slowed the engine and discussed with Jim a good place to anchor. He'd once sailed with William for a couple of seasons, he had said; and he didn't seem inclined to assume that he was the skipper, noted Sam with satisfaction. They decided on a clear circle of water amongst the twenty or thirty boats already anchored there.

'Let go anchor,' called her mother to Jim on the foredeck. She switched off the engine.

The air was hot and still, sheltered from the westerly outside. Sam gazed at the activity all around her: people swimming, diving, rowing dinghies, cruising in search of a place to anchor, or just sitting on their boats. A ferry was arriving, laden with people going to see Mansion House. It was all a dream, of course: that empty garden and deserted beach where she and Jane had run, angry and desperate, not so many hours before.

'The amphibian's coming into land. Look,' said Mrs Starr as the peace was broken by the mosquito buzz of the craft making a steep descent to touch down in the middle of the harbour.

'Someone arriving for the party tonight,' said her

mother. They watched the aircraft unload its passengers on the beach in front of Mansion House, then slip back into the water and roar off to another bay.

Some minutes later, Sam was the first to hear a gruff call. '*Aratika? Aratika!*'

Puzzled, she looked around. Many boats and people, yes, but no one she recognized.

'*Aratika!*' Over there in a dinghy, an old man with a bag across his knees and a floppy white sunhat on his head was being rowed towards them by a small boy.

'Here's William,' she said in astonishment.

'William who?' said her mother from the foot of the companion-way where she was preparing coffee.

'Grandfather William, of course.'

'What? What's he doing here? I had no idea he was coming to Kawau this weekend,' she said, climbing out into the cockpit to help the old man aboard. 'You look all ready for action.'

'I am. My fare, thanks, lad,' he said, bending down to give a coin to the small boy who had rowed him out. 'Well, that wasn't a bad flight, first time for me. Greetings, Jim,' he said to their crew. 'Haven't seen you for a while.'

'Why . . .?' began Mrs Starr.

'You had a rough ride last night, didn't you, Louise? Some problems.'

'Yes.'

'Where's Nick?'

'Gone to hospital,' said Sam, adding quickly 'but he's all right; it's just for a check-up and an X-ray. He's all right really.'

'What did he do? Hit himself over the head? Spinnaker pole? Chinese gybe?'

Sam looked at her mother. Perhaps she should do the talking now.

'Spinnaker pole,' said Mrs Starr. The old man nodded.

'I heard the wind get up, about ten, ten-thirty. Hardly slept a wink. I decided that you might be glad of an extra hand for the trip home tomorrow.'

'We certainly will,' said her mother warmly.

'So Nick's in hospital, eh? You two don't look too good, either. Where's Terry?' His pale eyes were taking in every detail of the condition of the boat as he lowered himself onto the cockpit seat. Sam could see his gaze rest for a long time on the bundle of spinnaker still lying dishevelled in the forepeak.

'It's a long story . . .' said Mrs Starr.

'Give me some coffee first, Louise. Then you can tell me.'

'How did you know, William?' said Sam.

'Intuition. It's something a wise sailor trusts. You can't sail a boat for fifty years, knowing every creak of her timbers, without knowing when something's wrong. Plain intuition, Sam.'

Sam looked across the deck at her mother. 'Something women are supposed to have lots of,' they said together and laughed until the sounds of their laughter echoed around the bay and were lost among the pine trees.

Glossary

New Zealand terms

Aratika   Maori name, meaning 'direct path'

bach   holiday cottage

chilly bin   insulated container

crook   sick

manuka   common scrub bush or tree (sometimes called tea-tree)

morepork   New Zealand owl

pavlova   dessert made of meringue topped with whipped cream and fruit

parka   anorak, jacket

pohutukawa   coastal evergreen tree with bright red flowers

puriri   hardwood tree

punga   tree-fern

tui   bird notable for its call and for the tuft of white feathers at its throat

weka   hen-sized flightless bird

Nautical terms

aback   sails pressed back against the mast or rigging by the wind

abeam   at right angles to a boat

amidships   middle

backstays   stays (wires) supporting mast from aft

beat (or tack)   to sail as close to the wind as possible

board   one zig of a zig-zag

boom   long spar used to keep the bottom of a sail extended

bowsprit   spar projecting from the bow of a boat to which jib and forestay are secured

burgee   triangular flag flown from mast

cleat   metal or wooden fitting to which a rope can be belayed (made fast); to make fast a rope around a cleat

clew   lower rear corner of sail

clinker   method of boat construction in which the planks of the hull overlap each other

coaming   raised border around the cockpit or hatch

cockpit   on a yacht, place in vicinity of tiller where helmsman and crew can sit, and from which sails are trimmed

companion-way   steps from cockpit down to cabin

fairlead   ring through which a sheet or warp is led

fairway   channel kept clear for vessels

fend off   to hold or push a boat away

forestay   wire stay from bow or bowsprit to support mast

204

genoa *large jib or headsail*

go about *change from one tack to another*

guy (spinnaker) *rope controlling spinnaker boom*

gybing *bringing the sail over to the opposite side by turning the boat's stern through the wind*

hatchway *entrance to cabin from cockpit or deck*

halyard *rope or wire used for hauling up sail*

hank *metal snaphook for attaching headsail to forestay*

head (of a sail) *the top of a sail, usually reinforced*

heel *to lean over under the pressure of wind or an uneven load*

helm *tiller or wheel*

in irons *when a sailing vessel lies head to wind and will not turn on either tack*

jib *the leading headsail*

keeler *New Zealand name for a yacht with a shaped weight or keel fastened below the hull to provide stability and to reduce leeway*

ketch *two-masted yacht with shorter mast aft*

kite *New Zealand term for spinnaker*

lee or leeward *side away from the wind; the lower side of a heeling yacht*

leech *trailing edge of sail*

lifelines *ropes attached to safety harnesses worn by crew, the lifeline then clipped to the rigging*

liferails *wires rigged through stanchions on the deck as a fence to prevent crew falling overboard*

luff *leading edge of a sail*

main *mainsail*

mainsheet *the rope which trims the mainsail*

painter *rope attached to bow of dinghy for towing or mooring*

pay off *when the head of the boat is moved away from the wind*

pinching *sailing too close to the wind*

port *the side of the boat to the left when facing for'ard (red navigation light)*

port tack *when the wind is coming over the port side and the boat is heeled over to the right*

pulpit *metal framework on the bow helping crew to work on the foredeck in safety*

reaching *sailing with the wind abeam (at right angles to the boat)*

shackle *metal fitting with a threaded pin to connect one piece of gear to another*

sheets *ropes which control the after corners of sails*

shrouds *wire stays which support the mast*

slip *to let go a mooring or warp*

spar   strong pole used to support a ship's sails

spinnaker   large lightweight sail used when reaching or running before the wind

spinnaker pole   boom holding a spinnaker away from the mast

spreaders   short horizontal arms holding shrouds clear of mast

stanchion   upright bar fixed around yacht's deck (see liferails)

starboard   the side of the boat to the right when facing for'ard (green navigation light)

starboard tack   when the wind is coming over the starboard side and the boat is heeled to the left

tack   another zig of a zig-zag. Also name for lower leading corner of sail

tacking   sailing to windward on a zig-zag course

thwarts   seats in a dinghy

tiller   horizontal bar, fixed to the rudder, by which most yachts are steered

uphaul   wire clipped to middle of spinnaker pole to control its angle

warp   rope used for anchoring and mooring

windward   side on which the wind is blowing; the higher side of a heeling yacht

Heard about the Puffin Club?

... it's a way of finding out more about Puffin books and authors, of winning prizes (in competitions), sharing jokes, a secret code, and perhaps seeing your name in print! When you join you get a copy of our magazine, *Puffin Post*, sent to you four times a year, a badge and a membership book.

For details of subscription and an application form, send a stamped addressed envelope to:

The Puffin Club Dept A
Penguin Books Limited
Bath Road
Harmondsworth
Middlesex UB7 0DA

and if you live in Australia, please write to:

The Australian Puffin Club
Penguin Books Australia Limited
P.O. Box 257
Ringwood
Victoria 3134